THE JAMES CHILDREN SERIES BOOK 1

KATHI S. BARTON

This is a work of fiction. Names, characters, places, and incidents are products of the author's imagination or are used factiously and are not to be construed as real. Any resemblance to actual events, locations, organizations, or person, living or dead, is entirely coincidental.

World Castle Publishing
Pensacola, Florida

Copyright © by Kathi S. Barton 2012
ISBN: 9781938243004
First Edition World Castle Publishing March 5, 2012
http://www.worldcastlepublishing.com

Cover: Karen Fuller
Photo: Shutterstock
Editor: Brieanna Robertson

~*Chapter 1*~

Jared Stone pulled up in front of the bar simply named "*Jim's*" at a quarter till one in the morning. He'd sat in his hotel room for over an hour and just wanted a beer and a few hours around people who spoke English for a change. The hotel staff, while very nice, just didn't cut it. He got out of his truck and went inside. He loved the place at first glance.

There were several televisions on, all to a game on Monday night football. The stools around the bar were evenly spaced and a little worn. Most of them were filled with butts that kept hopping up and down with the announcer on the television over the bar. The bar itself was a work of art, inlaid with different woods both light and dark to form a scene of the different highlights around Ohio, including the famous horseshoe stadium and a few buckeyes. There were several booths as well as half dozen or so tables with chairs scattered around the room. Jared could see a sectioned off area in the back and from the sounds, he thought it might be a pool room. He heard some shouting too, but ignored it as best he could as he sat up at the bar.

A young woman walked toward him while she rubbed down the bar. She looked barely old enough to be there and all Jared could think was he really needed to get out more.

"What'll you have? Got draft and menu's short tonight while the game is on." A crash and loud voices punctuated the cheers around the bar. The girl turned. "When your boss gets here, I hope you all get canned." Then under her breath, "Fucking construction workers."

Jared started to stand and go see the men in the back when the front door exploded open. In walked a blur of jeans, flannel, and dark hair. He looked back to the bartender when she yelled, "Catch." He watched as a Louisville Slugger sailed through the air and land in Flannel's hand. Jared was impressed. She hadn't even broken stride. Then he realized she was headed to the back room and he got up to follow her.

He watched as the woman slapped the bat under her arm and pulled a handful of her rich, dark hair up and off her neck. By the time she was steamrolling through the doorway, the bat was back in her hand and her hair was in a haphazard knot at the back of her head.

Jared got a nice view of what he considered a fine ass and shapely long legs before he lost her. By the time he got to the doorjamb where she had gone, he could see a dozen or so men standing around two pool tables. He could also see that most of them were wearing J.R. Stone Construction t-shirts. Jared stepped into the room to listen to her talk to his men.

"…nothing better to do at," she jerked her sleeve up and looked at the watch on her wrist, "one fucking o'clock in the morning than to come down here and babysit a bunch of overgrown idiots."

Jared nearly burst out laughing when every man dropped their heads and mumbled something to her.

"Donaldson, get Sherman and take him to the ER," she snapped. The sea of men parted to show a man sitting in one of the few booths with a bloodied towel at his head. Jared wondered how she'd seen the men. Even with her height, most of the men in front of the injured one were a good five to six inches taller.

"I'm okay, boss. Nothing more than—"

"Did you think I was requesting you to go? I was not. Donaldson, now. And tell the doc to send the bill to me. Understand?"

A burly man broke from the standing pack and helped the injured Sherman up and out the door. Jared got a good look at the cut as they went by him and was surprised that the man was standing. The men shuffled again. He would bet she wasn't finished.

"Conley, tell me what happened. And you aren't reciting *War and Peace*. Short informative sentences will do."

"Well now," Conley started, and moved to the front of the pack. "Sherman there was playing a game of pool with Talbor, Denny, and me. He was winning. Sank the eight in—" A sharp look from Miss Flannel had him straighten up. "Sherman was winning and Talbor there got pissy. Said we was cheating."

"He fucking was. I seen him—" The bat raised so quickly that Jared was sure it had been spring loaded. The man speaking, Talbor, Jared assumed, snarled at her.

"When it's your turn you can wow me with your side." Her voice was low and calm but full of venom. "I'm listening to Conley and you will shut the fuck up. Conley?"

"Talbor started yelling about suing. Sherman ignored him. You know how he can do that. Can talk to the man all day and it's like he ain't heard a word. But he's listening, he can—" This time, she slapped the bat in her hand. "Sorry,

Will. Anyway, when Sherman didn't fight back, Talbor hit him with his stick."

The woman turned toward Talbor now. "I've had about all you I can take, Talbor. Tomorrow morning, you stay off my site. I don't want—"

Her head snapped back from the blow. Talbor's fist shot out so fast no one could have prevented it. Jared was two steps in when Miss Flannel leapt forward and hit Talbor back. Her fist hit him in the nose and blood spurted forward. Then in a move that Jared was both impressed and startled by, she had the bat around the man's throat and him on the floor in front of her.

Talbor held it from his neck with both hands as blood stained the front of his shirt. The muscles in his forearms were bunched and corded trying to push it away, showing the girl was as strong as she was gutsy.

"You're going to pay for this, bitch," he snarled at her. "When my daddy finds out, he'll yank your permits so quick that that fucker Stone won't have no choice but to fire your tight fucking ass. I've been talking to him you know? Stone. He ain't no happier about you than anybody else is."

Jared stopped his forward motion. This was why he was here. His father had called him home from the job site in Paris to come here to fire his foreman. Jared had a sneaky suspicion that Will James was the woman before him and not the man his father thought she was.

She let Talbor go and he fell forward. She stepped around him and Jared got his first look at Miss Flannel.

Her eye was swollen shut and her lip was bleeding. Blood stained her shirt front too. One of the men standing there stopped her from falling or Jared wasn't sure what she would have done. When she turned back to him again, he took a breath. Even bloodied and beat up, she was beautiful. Jared was suddenly glad that he had been sent to Ohio.

~o0o~

Willow looked at her men. She was exhausted and hurting. All she wanted to do was sit down on one of the numerous stools and bawl, bawl like a little baby. But it wouldn't solve the problems she was now dealing with.

"You all have ten minutes to clean this mess up and set the room to rights. I want this floor cleaned and chairs put back where they were." She leaned against the pool table, careful not to get her blood in the green felt. "If you aren't on time tomorrow, I will dock you an hour's pay. You don't show…then I suggest you use your day off wisely and find another gig."

She turned away and noticed the man standing there, but ignored him. A patron of the bar had come to see the show, she figured. When Talbor started in again on suing her and Stone Construction, she stood up, left the room, and went to the bar where Lindsey was. Willow handed her the bat back, took the bag of ice, and put it on her eye.

"Bastard outta be locked up. His daddy's been bailing his ass out for more'n ten years." Willow nodded. "You hurt much?" Lindsey asked her.

"Enough." Willow pulled her credit card out of her back pocket and slid it across the bar. "Run this for damages. Don't worry your insurance company. They'll just raise your rates anyway. I'm sorry about this, Lins."

Willow noticed the man from the doorway slide back onto a stool about midway down the bar. Willow couldn't see much of him because of the shadows. She could only see that he was tall and dark-haired.

"Sorry about this, Will, but you know Durk the Jerk. If I don't get some money, he'll make me pay it outta my own pocket." Lindsey gave her back the card.

Willow knew that and also that Lindsey would only charge what she thought was fair. Her boss, Durk Josephs, would double whatever he thought he could get out of Willow.

Willow looked down at her credit card. Willow D. James, it said, and she wondered every time she used it who that girl was. She was a long way from that rich girl who was named there. Moving toward the door, Willow followed her men out the door.

Some of them would follow her home. She knew they would no matter what she told them to do. She didn't bother. She was tired and her head was pounding. Sliding under the steering wheel of her truck, she started up and headed home.

Willow loved her house. She'd bought it ten years ago just after she started working for Stone. She'd only been a gopher then. Fetching coffee and nails, bringing equipment to the other men, whatever they needed. Tony Ranch had been the foreman then and had been a bastard and treated her like shit. It wasn't until a year later that he'd been promoted and Tommy Patel had been promoted into his position. That's when she had started working on the site as a worker and not some slave to Ranch.

Willow had been going to school then. At nineteen, she was in her last year of a business degree with one more year of architectural design. She already had a landscaping degree from attending college while in high school. Her parents loved her so they indulged what they thought of as a whim. She smiled when she thought about the day she'd gotten her first site job and how they had tried to hide their disappointment. Her brother Alexander had been the one to tell them that she would be brilliant at it. She secretly thought they had hoped she would grow bored with it and move on to more feminine projects. She hadn't. And now, if one asked them, they would tell people it had been their idea all along. Her smile reminded her of her split lip.

Turning on the lights in her bedroom, she heard the vehicle that had followed her home drive away. She was in the bathroom a few minutes later. She looked at her watch and discovered it was just shy of two-thirty. Fuck, she was tired. Debating whether to shower and stay up or go have her lip stitched, she turned on the water. No reason she couldn't do both. By three, she was sitting on a gurney waiting for the nurse to come in and sew her up.

"Want to explain how a woman I know never took a drink in her life gets her lip split in a bar fight? Or do you have some extra sideline work going on that I'm not aware of?"

Willow rolled to her back when Shannon Weiss came in with a small arsenal of medical supplies. "Nope. Just building buildings. Talbor did it."

"Ah. Say no more." Shannon shook her head. "Punk-assed bastard. Why don't you fire him? He's gotta have a file a mile wide by now. And what's he worked for you now…six, seven months?"

"Five. But I can't. The last time I tried, our permits were yanked for nine days. Stone was pissed. Said I either make it work or else he'd find someone who would." Willow shrugged. "So I'm making it work."

She didn't say anything while her mouth was being stitched. The Novocain made it difficult anyway. So she just closed her eyes.

She used to like coming to work. At least until Stone moved away to the warmer climates during the colder months—not that she'd ever met him. All their conversations had been through emails. Willow supposed that the Carolinas weren't all that far, but it wasn't like the big boss was all that close either. She felt herself drifting off and with a raised hand to stall Shannon, she asked her to wake her when she was finished.

~Chapter 2~

Jared woke at ten in the morning. He was groggy and a little disorientated, but came awake quickly. He was out of the shower and dressed by ten-thirty, waiting on breakfast. He decided he needed a house, or at the very least somewhere he could have his own kitchen.

He thought about where he wanted to stay and realized he could move into his parents' house while he tried to figure it out. He would have all the comforts without all the strangeness of it all. He made a mental note to clear it with his dad when he spoke to him tonight.

Jared had planned on going to the site on Monday of the next week. That would have given him four days and the weekend to sort out living arrangements and set up appointments with Talbor and Will James. Jared smiled when he thought of "Will."

His father had assumed she was a he. So had Jared, actually. But he was a she, and a very lovely she at that. When she had left the bar, he thought about following her home, but three men that had left when she did made him rethink that. Jared wisely thought he could handle one man, but three? Well, he wasn't that stupid. Besides, he had her file on his desk.

Picking up the file now, Jared skimmed over her impressive records and degrees. Not only was Miss James qualified to do her job, she might be considered over-qualified by many. Then he picked up the file his dad's secretary had handed him at the airport when he'd landed yesterday morning.

"We have had numerous letters from Ranch, a former site foreman, and the city council. Mr. Talbor is claiming that W. James is not bringing the building up to standard and that the men are a nuisance in the city at nights. We also have a letter...we quite a few from one of our employees stating that W. James is forcing all the men to have sex with him in exchange for extra pay."

Jared smiled at that. He didn't care about anyone's sexual preference, but Talbor was claiming that Foreman James was forcing them to do so. Mr. James might have raised a brow or two, but Jared highly doubted there was a man alive who wouldn't feel it a great honor to have to sleep with Miss James. But that accusation was just one of the many things on his list of things to check out. His cell phone was ringing when he was leaving the hotel. His mom.

"So, how is the jet-setting Stone boy getting along? Seduced any women yet? Or should I just ask how many?"

"It's only noon, Mom. I've only been able to move through the hotel staff so far. But I have a request for them to bring in the older babes later, just for an aperitif." Jared laughed when she huffed at him. "How are the beaches? Enjoying yourself?"

"Yes, but I miss you. Come down for a visit this week. We'll go on a clam bake. The neighbor's daughter is visiting and she is a pretty single thing."

Jared wondered what his mother would think of Willow and frowned. He didn't care what she thought of her. He was here to do a job, not date the help, even if she was very beautiful. Deciding to ignore her not so stubble hints at matrimony, he asked her about the house.

"Of course stay there. I'm sorry I didn't think to tell you to stay there anyway. The staff is still there…mostly anyway. Beard is there and I'll tell him to hire what you'll need to fill in." He could hear her clicking a pen to make herself notes as she continued. "I'll call her when we get off here. How's it going otherwise? Have you gotten any sleep?"

"I'm fine. I have some things I need to work out at the site. Then I have a couple of things I'm going to have to do at the office for tomorrow. Dad said he left things in the air about the foreman and for me to handle it as I saw fit." Jared threw the file on the seat next to him. "Mom, who do you know who would be able to do some research on a couple of people?"

"Sara Kensal is your father's lawyer. She would know most everyone we do. If it's social background, maybe I can help. Who is it?"

Jared debated. He figured his mom would have heard about Shawn Talbor. He'd been on a campaign to have the foreman fired for over three months, according to his dad. But it was Willow he was actually wondering about. His mother would know if she'd been in trouble on a site before and anything she might have done before Stone. He decided to hold off on Willow and get what he could about the Talbors.

"Shawn Sr. is on the city council. He's a pompous ass, if you ask me. About three years ago, he thought it would be a good idea to cut the city bus drivers pay by one third. He didn't tell them and when they got their next check, they were in an uproar about it." His mother laughed. "They drove the buses to his house and parked them all over his lawn when he wouldn't return their calls. My goodness, that was funny."

Jared could almost see his mom sitting at her little desk telling him this story. He smiled at the thought.

"And Mrs. Talbor? What do you know about her?"

The sobered reply came immediately. "She passed on several years ago. Some say she killed herself, others said she died of a broken heart."

Like her humor, he could see her in sorrow too. He decided to change the subject quickly. He moved on to his trip to come there and see them. Toward the end of the call, he asked his mother about his plan in dealing with the situation here in Ohio.

"I'll just show up as an employee. I'll have Sara set it up that I'm to be hired on. I believe getting both sides of this would go better in the long run. If what you say is true about the Talbor family, then maybe the apple doesn't fall far from the tree."

"If you show up as Jared Stone, you think anyone is going to connect the dots? Not all of them can be as stupid as this Talbor is," his mother said. "Go by Jared Robert. It's still your name and it's common enough that no one will give it a second thought."

Jared was glad he'd told her about it. He would never have thought about changing his name until someone asked him for it. Then he would have been stuck.

"Okay. Then I'll start this Monday. I'm going to move my stuff over to the house today when I get back." he tried to think if he was forgetting anything. "Mom, thanks. I'll see you in a couple of days. No matchmaking while I'm down there, all right?"

She huffed at him again. "It's my right to be matchmaker. And until I'm holding Jared the sixth on my knee, I'll continue to do so. I'll see you in a few days. I love you, Jared, be careful."

The rest of his day was filled with moving his things to the house, making arrangements with a realtor, setting up appointments with the people he'd need to see at the firm, and packing for a few days at his parents' house.

Jared had been in Paris for the past eighteen months overseeing a huge construction site there. The mall they were building had been riddled with one issue after another— shorted supplies and not enough staff to complete the job were just a few of the problems. Jared had been sent over to see what the real problem was. He'd found more than they'd bargained for.

The foreman was a thief. Not just with the Stone supplies, but even a ring of house thefts had been linked to him and almost half the crew. Jared caught on to it the second day he had been there.

Then they were behind schedule, which put them over budget. By the time he'd gotten there, walls should have been up and foundation poured for flooring. Half the walls up had to be torn down and redone. And none of the foundations were worked enough to even begin the pouring process. It had taken the first five weeks just to get a crew organized and another ten weeks of working seventy hours just to get back on track.

They were way over budget now, but going to finish on time. The foreman was in jail along with seven of the crew and indictments for another five. The man he'd left in charge was going to do a great job. Jared decided he was going to enjoy a few days with his parents and forget work and everything else.

~o0o~

Tuesday morning, the city inspector, the city councilman, Talbor, and his son were on site when Willow pulled up at seven o'clock. She was half tempted to just start her truck back up and go home. When she got out, all of them approached her. She didn't even slow as she walked past them.

"Gentlemen, Talbor." She didn't really think any of them were even close to being gentlemen, but she said it anyway. She didn't stop walking until she was inside her office and shut the door in their faces. Then she turned the tab to lock the door behind her. Leaning against it, she realized that other than leaving at night, it was the first time the lock had been engaged since she'd been on this site. Ignoring the knocks, then the pounding, she set about opening her emails and forwarding on to the company attorney anything she didn't know what to do with. Sarah Kensal usually handled all of it anyway. At three minutes until eight, someone unlocked the door and came inside.

"Morning," Tommy Conley said when he walked in. "Got yourself quite a crowed out here, boss. You gonna hide—mother fuck. Is that what Talbor did to you last night?"

Willow had been surprised herself when she'd gotten a look in the hand mirror that Shannon had given her when Willow had woke up. Her lip was swollen and the eight tight black stitches stood out in sharp contrast against her fair skin. Her eye had four stitches across the brow. Shannon had put them in when Willow had been asleep or she wouldn't have allowed her to do it. Willow's eye was puffy, but not as swollen this morning. However, she couldn't put ice packs on it so she was sure it looked bad again.

"Talbor has a nice right. Hopefully, he doesn't look any better this morning." Willow hadn't really looked at him when she'd gotten out of her truck. She had just wanted to get away from them as soon as possible. She stood up now to go out and talk to them.

Conley stopped her with a hand to her arm. "You're gonna have to take him back, aren't you?" She nodded. "That fucking sucks, you know that, right?"

Yes, it did. But she wasn't going to lose her job over an asshole like Talbor.

~Chapter 3~

Jared was ready to begin work by Monday. Actually, he'd decided to head out when he returned to Ohio on Sunday afternoon. He was surprised when he got there that there was a truck in the parking lot. He could see someone in the site trailer, but didn't know who so he parked on the street and walked around the yard and building shell.

The walls were in, but only some of the interior wiring was finished on the third floor office building. Jared knew from the weekly reports that the electricians were due to bring in extra crew to finish the job by the end of the week. Bricking off the outside of the façade was nearly done with just one more wall nearly to completion. Going in through one of the boarded up doors, he stepped into a large, open area.

The building was slated for a single company and the drywall was being put up to make the individual rooms on the lower floors. Most of the first floor wasn't finished so he walked to the stairs to go to the top floors and make his way down. He smiled when he got to the second level.

Stone prided itself on the way they finished a building. The crews would finish the top floors first then work down and out. He noticed that the upper floor, the topmost level, was just awaiting mud work on the seams of the hung drywall. In the four rooms up here, two of them had been painted and of those, one had the ceiling completed. Jared was touring the second floor when he was stopped by a deep, hard voice.

"You got a reason to be hanging around a closed construction site? 'Cause if not, then I suggest you get the fuck outta here."

Jared turned around slowly. He didn't know the man behind him and didn't know what the man might have pointed at him, like another bat or a gun. Jared was surprised to see two people standing there. One was the man from the bar; Conley, if he remembered correctly. The other was Willow.

His first thought was that she looked exhausted, then he noticed her face. Christ, she was bruised. He caught himself before he went to her. Then he really took a better look.

She was taller than he remembered at about five-foot, ten inches. She was also very beautiful. Even with her bruised eye and lip, she still looked like every man's dream, both sexy and innocent at the same time. Her eyes were clear, a shade of blue so light that he knew they were as unique as the woman was. A small patrician nose and high cheekbones gave the impression of a model, but for some reason, Jared knew she'd scoff at the notion. Willow's hair was pulled back again; its rich, dark color looked blue-black under the harshness of the bulbs hanging from unfinished fixtures.

Today she had on just a t-shirt and jeans; the flannel, he realized now, had hidden a great deal of the woman. Full breasts strained the shirt and her muscled arms looked like she was a working foreman rather than an office one. Her jeans hung low on her full hips and curved over her thighs like a second skin. Tears at the knees and one at the thigh were not from some manufacturer's idea of what worn jeans looked like, but from actual work. Jared found himself wanting to ask her to turn around so that he could see if her ass looked as good as he remembered. Conley clearing his throat had Jared look back at him. He knew in that moment that the other man knew just where Jared's thought had been.

"I start working here tomorrow. I'm Jared Robert." He reached for his wallet, suddenly glad he'd had new identities made with his partial name on them. "Miss Kensal set it up. I was just seeing where I'd be working."

Conley took his driver's license and with a quick glance, handed it to Willow. She looked, but made no comment as she handed it back to Jared.

"I'm Will James, the foreman here. This is my second in command, Thomas Conley." She cocked her head at him. "You were at the bar last weekend...Monday, in the back room when..." She looked up at Conley.

"Yeah. I'd just come home from another job. I'm here to fill in work until the job is complete. You should have been notified sometime last week that I was coming." At least he hoped so.

"Yeah, got it Friday. Work begins here at eight on Monday, Robert, not Sunday afternoon. You're lucky no one shot you. Conley, show Robert the lay of the land then both of you get the hell off my job site. I got shit to do and I don't need a babysitter." Willow looked pointedly at Conley and he smiled back at her.

"Okay, boss. But you'll call if you...you know." She nodded at Conley and left them standing there.

Jared and Conley stood watching each other until they heard the board move back over the opening again. It was quiet for a full minute before Conley spoke.

"She ain't gonna like that you lied to her. She's real big on honesty." Jared didn't say anything, but was shocked. "You and I met about five years ago at a company function. You here to fire her or to congratulate her?"

A man that got to the heart of things. Jared liked him instantly. "Neither, for now. I'm here to work, like I said, and to see what's going on. We've gotten a few...quite a few complaints about her." Jared studied the man standing before him. "Are you going to tell her?"

Conley looked down the stairs before answering. "Nope. Not my place. But I won't help you either. Don't come to me about information on her. I won't help you either way. But know this, if she asks me, I will tell her." Conley looked down the stairs again. "If you want my opinion, I think sending in a spy for your old man is about as low as it comes. I'm sure you know your way around your own site, Robert." And with that, he left.

The same dirty truck was in the lot the next morning. There were any number of others there, a car and two motorcycles as well. Jared wasn't sure which vehicle was Willow's or Conley's, but he parked next to a truck that made him wonder if the driver lived it in. There were enough fast food wrappers and cola cans that he was sure they could fill a large land fill. With a shake of his head, he went to the trailer where several men and Willow were standing. It was just past seven-thirty.

"...Sherman on floor two. I want those walls primed for Wednesday A.M. when the painters get here. Viktor and Jacobs, you're to get the ceilings done on the top floor. There are..." Willow looked down at the clip board in her hand

24

before she continued. "Seven on the second and the entire entrance this week. If you have time, I want you to begin the second floor as well. There are some more lights that go in there that the owner had decided to add. This is Robert, Jared Robert, and he'll be with Thomason and Ruby on the set of the stone in the main entrance and office of the president. The rest of you get the drywall hung. Anything else?"

"You didn't assign me nothing, boss." The voice was heavy with scorn and he had sneered her title like it was a dirty word. Jared turned to see the man behind him.

He knew who he was, Talbor. The man had both his eyes still blackened, but probably not as bad as it had been. Jared wanted to laugh at the squat man, but didn't want to get off on the wrong foot this early in the job.

"Have you finished the clean up?" Willow didn't look at her list for him. "I told you on Tuesday and then Wednesday that was your job until it was complete. I was told I had to work you. Doesn't mean I have to find you something constructive you can fuck up. Now you—"

"I ain't no fucking maid service. You put me to work inside, out of the sun, or I'll tell my daddy that you ain't complying to the arrangement." Jared, as did everyone else, turned back to the man. "You ain't fucking gonna get away with this soon as Stone finds out what I have to tell him."

Willow laughed at the man's threat. "You ever get tired of that same litany every time you don't get your way, Talbor? Your daddy bailing your ass out all the time? Clean up or I'll cite you for failure to do your job."

She walked away even as he kept the insults up. The men didn't say anything either, but simply went to their assigned jobs. Jared wasn't sure if she had told them not to speak or they just didn't care. At this point, he wasn't sure what to think either. He followed the two men who went into the building to the main hall.

Laying stone was usually left for a mason on a building site. Jared had been taught how to lay the stone when he'd still been in high school and knew that it was on his application that Willow had received from Sarah. He was really good at it too. He knew from the file on the men working here that both the men he was working with were masons and they wasted no time getting set up and to work.

The sub flooring had already been sectioned off into four even squares with a snap chalk line. It started at the middle of each of the four walls and met in the center of the room to form a large X. It would be the starting point for them to work with.

Ruby set Jared to work spreading the mortar after he asked Jared if he'd ever done it before. Jared had the thin-set mortar spread over about a four foot square area. The mortar needed to be in a combed pattern so they could follow the lines in the floor to keep the lines straight. As the men began laying the design of colored stone tile, putting spacers between each one to keep an even grout line, they began to talk.

"You gonna be replacing one of us or you just here to fill in? Got my hopes on the first part so long as it ain't me, you understand."

Ruby sounded like he hailed from the Deep South. There was a soft cadence about his voice that was soothing and funny at the same time. Jared knew he was from Atlanta and that Thomason, the other man, was from California.

"Nah. Just helping out. I've been out of town for a while and this gig came up so I jumped on it." his cover story was as close to the truth as he could give without giving away who he was. "I was missing home so I thought what the hell."

The men worked in silence for the most part after that. Twice he heard Willow's voice and once he'd caught a glimpse of her as she strode by the room, but she never stopped to speak to them. He was impressed that she didn't micromanage her people, but for a reason he didn't want to think about, was aggravated that she didn't. They were breaking for lunch when he saw her again.

She was directing a delivery truck to one of the many site storage units. It was a tractor trailer loaded with drywall and buckets of what he assumed was plaster. He watched her as she walked over to a forklift and strapped in when the truck was parked. As she began to unload the heavy pallets, Jared felt someone come up behind him and wasn't surprised that it was Shawn Talbor.

"She's a fucking bitch, you know. Thinks her shit don't stink. I fucking hate her." his voice was low but full of hatred.

Without turning around, Jared asked him, "Then why do you work here? Seems to me there are plenty of other construction companies around you could sign on with. Most or all of them would welcome someone from Stone Construction."

Which wasn't true. Word was that Stone was difficult to get hired on to, but if you left on your own, you were either stupid or retiring. Jared knew that they paid top dollar and treated their employees with respect.

The answering laugh sent a chill down Jared's spine. "'Cause it would make her day. I'll stick around. 'Sides, Daddy said if I play my cards right, I'll have her job before much longer. But she's been fucking that old man Stone for years and got herself buried in like a tick. Only reason she got this far is 'cause she gives good head."

Jared didn't turn now because had he done so, he would have killed the man. His parents were the most faithful people he knew and his father had never had an affair. He knew this because his mother told him that as long as he was alive, then she knew this for a fact. She claimed, and Jared didn't doubt her, that no one would ever find his body if he even thought about having one.

"Course you can ask any man here about that too. 'Specially Conley. Them two been going at it for months. Heard tell she prefers married men to the single ones. Why I don't stand a chance with her, not that I'd touch some man's seconds." With that and his maniacal laughter, he left Jared to go to the lunch wagon.

Jared ate with the other men. Willow emptied the flatbed while they did. Most watched her; a couple of them wandered over then came back. Jared wondered if they set up duties or offered to help. He wasn't sure why what Talbor said bothered him so much. It wasn't as if he was dating her or anything. After lunch, he went to the upper floors before going back to work on the tile.

The second floor had been less than a quarter finished with hanging the drywall last night. Today all but one wall was hung and it was being done now. Willow was setting a screw to the last one as he stood watching her.

~o0o~

Willow had a set of headphones on and was listening to a book. She didn't particularly care for music, but needed something to drown out the constant hammering and other things going on. It really was too bad the book wasn't working.

When she got the last sheet into place and the last screw set, she turned to get her pail and trowel. She was startled to see the new guy there. She pulled off the headphones.

"Something I can help you with, Robert?" She looked around and found they, for the most part, were coming along. "You just looking around again?"

He'd been leaning against the doorjamb, but straightened now. There was something about the man that made her nervous. It wasn't his height, though that was impressive at about six-foot-six. It was something...manly, she thought, that made her feel weird. He looked like one of those guys on the cover of one of the books, Shasta, her mother's cook, read. She called them bodice rippers and the men looked like they could take on the world.

"No," he said as he moved closer. "I was just wondering what you're doing. Didn't see you at lunch and thought maybe you had a picnic or something up here."

Willow wanted desperately to back away, but stood her ground. "No, just me. I don't usually stop for...shouldn't you be on the tile job?" Anywhere but here, she thought.

He reached up and plucked at her hair and showed her the plaster he'd removed. "We're waiting on the stone to be delivered. Supposed to be on the way."

Willow nodded as she watched his fingers roll the plaster between them. His fingers were incredibly long and so slender. She couldn't help but think about them touching her. And her skin heated. This man worked for her. She looked up at his face when his fingers stopped moving.

It was a beautiful face, strong jaw line, straight, narrow nose. The stubble on his face was dark and begged to be touched to see if it was soft or hard. His eyes were a dark brown, like hot cocoa made with melted dark chocolate rather than with cocoa. His hair was a warm brown and curly at the ends. He wore it long and he had it pulled to the nape of his neck in a pony tail that was probably six inches long. His voice, when he spoke to her now, was dark, low, and made her body tingle.

"How's your mouth, Willow?" He ran his thumb over her lower lip and asked her again.

"Fine. Sore. I've had worse." She took a step back then another when he stepped toward her. "You should go back to work." Her own voice was like nothing she'd ever heard before.

She didn't know what he might have said, but a shout from the lower level had them both back apart. Willow had never been so glad for the noise in her life.

~Chapter 4~

Willow avoided him completely on Tuesday and Wednesday. On Thursday, she had to take the morning off to have the stitches removed and didn't get to work until after eleven. By the time she'd caught up on her mail and fielding calls from vendors, she was nearly five hours behind. At six o'clock, the last truck left the lot and she was on the first floor covering seams with mud on the newly hung drywall.

She'd thought about Robert all week and wondered for the hundredth time what he'd been about to do. Kiss her? She certainly would have let him at that moment and gotten angry with herself all over. No matter how appealing it was, kissing her employees was out of the question. If it ever was a possibility. She snorted to herself and turned the volume up on her book.

It was nearly eleven when she got to her house. Exhausted and dirty, she stripped down to her boxer briefs and bra in the kitchen and tossed the whole load in the washer. One more day, she thought. Then she'd have two days off in a row. Then she remembered her dinner date with her parents.

"Fuck, fuck fuck." Standing in the kitchen listening to the washer fill, Willow wondered if she could get out of it. She was running ideas through her head when her phone rang. It was one of her parents, as they were the only ones with this number.

"Hello, parental unit. How's it hanging?" She smiled when her father sputtered on the other end.

"You ever check your messages, young lady? Your mother has been frantic."

Willow smiled bigger. Her mother didn't get frantic, her dad did. "I've been having a torrid affair with the milk man and he keeps strange hours. He had to keep me a secret from his wife and eight kids."

Willow burst out laughing at her dad's "smart ass," but he went on without any more comments about her mom. "This dinner thing tomorrow night, I'll expect you here on time and without a stitch of flannel on. Ghastly attire you've gotten into the habit of wearing." There went her hopes of getting out of it.

"I had a dress made of just that material too. Now what will I wear? Maybe if you're really nice to me and tell me the name of the man mom and you have set me up with this time, I'll know what to wear." She had a number of clothes that would deter even the quickest hands.

Her dad snorted, a nice habit she'd taught him to do. "Your mother has two set up. Well, one from each of us. Miscommunication or some other stupid reason. I distinctly remember her telling me to invite young Nathan, but now she swears that she didn't. That ugly boy Taylor is coming too."

Willow laughed. "He's not ugly, Dad. He's unique." Boy was he ever.

"Willow, the man has the biggest ears I've ever seen. Why, in a good storm, a wind would pick him up and he'd be on the space station in a matter of minutes. And that laughter…sounds like a bull horn going off."

Willow did agree about the laughter, but could only laugh more. She loved her parents very much and was a daddy's girl too. She and her mom had been best friends since she'd discovered, at age ten, that her mother hid a wicked sense of humor and a sharp wit. They had never had the usual problems most families had. Willow even enjoyed the company of her older brother Alexander.

"So," she stretched out the word. "I suppose you'd probably prefer it if I didn't marry Taylor. And since Nathan won't have me, then I guess I'm safe for the night."

Willow waited for the explosion and wasn't disappointed. "What do you mean he 'won't have you?' Why that man would be damned lucky if you gave him the time of day. Won't have you—why, men would be lining up if you'd pay them the slightest attention. Why won't he have you? I'll tear him apart for saying such a thing."

"Because, my dearest defender, I don't have the equipment he prefers in a sexual partner. And I'm pretty sure he has one. A partner, I mean."

The silence at the other end was profound. She opened the icebox and waited while she tried to remember the last time Marta, her housekeeper, friend, and cook, had bought groceries.

Marta Priest was due back tomorrow, thank goodness. Willow had missed her while she'd been on vacation. But putting up with Willow, she figured the woman needed a break.

The house seemed incredibly empty and not just of food, but also Marta's sage advice and her smart-assed answers. Marta was the daughter of Willow's parents' cook, Shasta.

Her dad, she knew, was sorting thought the information no doubt trying to figure out a way to still marry her off. She knew he wouldn't care about Nathan being gay. That had nothing to do with either their friendship, or hers to him for that matter. But he would try to salvage something out of this.

"Willow, honey, where do you get—never mind. I'm sure as your father I just don't want to know." The heavy sigh made her smile. "All right then, we'll just be a bunch of friends and family getting together. Your brother is going to try and make it in, but he said he couldn't guarantee anything at this point. And you stay away from that Taylor boy. I won't have you getting with child by him. Birthing one of his children with those ears could kill you."

Willow hung up a little while later after her dad went on then about her brother and how her mother despaired of the day he'd have a baby. She didn't even tell him that Alex having a child would be harder than her birthing Taylor's kid, but let it go.

She was too tired to even open a can of soup, had there been one in the house to do so. She was trudging up the stairs to her bedroom when she decided she'd go to the store Saturday on her way home if Marta didn't. Pulling a small pad of paper and a pen to her as she laid down, she made a note of things to get. She hated shopping for food almost as much as she hated to do laundry. Which was why, she thought with a huge yawn, she had about seventy pairs of underwear and that many t-shirts too. She fell asleep with the pen still in her hand along with the pad of sticky notes.

When she woke the next morning at four, she was covered in sticky notes and ink blotches. As she stripped off her sheets, she made herself a mental note to buy pencils and then discarded that idea almost immediately. It would be just her luck she'd end up with lead poisoning if she slept with a pencil. After taking a long shower, she made her way to the closet.

Willow had purchased the house at an estate auction. Her parents had helped her get the loan. Even with all her money and a job, the bank didn't want to loan money to a then seventeen-year-old kid. But she had paid the loan back on time and had also been able to get a second loan on her own since then.

The house for the most part had been in great shape. The lawns were the worst she'd ever seen, but she'd enjoyed bringing them back to life. All the bushes had to be pulled up and instead of replacing them as the local nursery had suggested, Willow planted bulbs and perennials and flowering fruit trees. She had made the cover of Architectural Digest last fall for her grounds alone.

The yard in the back had been useless so Willow had had a large in-ground pool put in along with a pool house and a little cottage for Marta to live in. Willow spent a great deal of time in the back yard in the warmer months and even the cooler ones since she'd had the pool heated. Willow simply loved the outdoors.

The third floor of the house was finished, as it was where her room was. The original house had had four bedrooms on the third floor and six on the second with a single bathroom per floor. Now after three years, there was a master suite complete with fireplace, sitting area, and an office. Both bedrooms had massive bathrooms as well.

The master bath had a large shower stall, as well as a sunken tub. She loved its jets and when she was able to use it, lit candles to set all around the glass block shelves that formed the outside wall. The toilet and sink were separated from the tub by another wall of glass blocks. She'd had to order the porcelain in the room, as it was a dark cobalt blue, so that the sink, toilet, counter top, and tub all were dark against the blue and white tile of the floor. The shower stall was surrounded in the glass and some had been filled with a blue gas that seemingly moved inside. As one stepped back toward the bedroom, there was a closet complete with dresser that sat back to back to each other. They split the room in half and divided the closet perfectly.

She hadn't wanted to put in two dressers, but her mother pointed out that if she ever sold the house to buy something bigger or something to play with, she would have a better chance of selling it for a couple.

Willow loved her bedroom with its twelve foot ceilings and top to bottom windows. The two outside walls both had two each. Since there was no need for a closet in this room, Willow built the headboard into the wall and made sure it had all the comforts she wanted, including the size of the custom mattress at one and a half the size of a regular king. The small end tables pulled out and there was a gun safe behind one and a fire proof safe behind the other. She had them both filled with her things. Most nights when she came home from work, it was all she could do to put the gun back in the safe because she never left the site until well after dark.

There was a gas fireplace in the wall directly across from the bed and a sofa and two wing backed chairs as well. There was also a work area, though Willow never used it, but it had been a suggestion from her dad and since she let her mom talk her into the double dressers, she went with the workstation to appease the man. He had blustered for days about it.

The other bedroom, only marginally smaller than the one she slept in, had the same type of headboard, but there was no bed. She used that room strictly for storage and nothing more. After she was dressed, Willow went to her office.

The second floor had taken her the most time. It had been her plan to reduce the number of bedrooms down to two as well, but had taken out two of the rooms and added baths that each set of bedrooms shared. She'd taken out the smallish closets and replaced them with large walk-ins that were well-lit and spacious.

The bedrooms were finished for the most part. Carpet had been taken up and the floor sanded and finished. But the woodwork, wide ceiling molding, and overhead fans needed to be hung, and the furniture, all antiques, had to be put back in place. Most of it was in storage in the garage.

The first floor had a grand entrance with wide double doors and stained glass windows down either side of it. The parquet floors replaced the worn tile and Willow had talked her parents into the beautiful chandelier she'd wanted for the ceiling last Christmas.

There was a huge living room that was devoid of anything—not even pictures on the wall. She didn't spend any time in there so was in no rush to furnish it.

The dining room was big enough to hold the cherry and walnut table she'd bought with its fourteen chairs and the massive hutch that held some of her collection of snowmen. She didn't use this room much either.

There was her office, which had been the first room finished, and she thought it reflected her tastes perfectly. A hodgepodge, her mother had called it, but Willow loved it. This room was as big if not bigger than some living rooms, though smaller than the two bedrooms in the house. The computer desk had been custom built by her and stained and polished by her dad. The desk was a rich cherry and shone brightly in the sunny room. The wall over the desk and down both sides held shelves and a filing cabinet each. The shelves were overflowing with books of all kinds, styles, and genres.

Willow was an eclectic reader and her books reflected that. Alongside signed first editions were dog-eared paperbacks as well as comic books and magazines. She simply loved the written word.

The kitchen was mostly complete and would be as soon as Marta told her what else it needed. Willow didn't cook, hated the task so much so that she would gladly live off pizza and take out before she'd ever try her hand at it. She and her dogs spent most of their time when she was home in the family room off from the kitchen.

By just after seven, she was just finishing up with her last email when someone knocked at her door. Not expecting anyone or anything, she went to the door and opened it, ready to blast anyone who dared bother her on a Friday morning. With a squeal of delight, she launched herself into her brother's chest.

~o0o~

Jared wandered through the house the realtor was showing him. This one, like the other four he'd been through, wasn't what he wanted. He wasn't sure what that was, but this wasn't it. He came down the stairs no longer listening to the man…something Jones was clattering on about the houses charms.

Jared had a mental list. Number one on the list was a large kitchen—a large, working kitchen. One he could move around in, entertain if he wanted, and to make love on the counter if Willow was in the mood.

The realtor, William, Jared suddenly remembered, bumped into him when he suddenly stopped. Willow in the mood? Where the hell had that come from?

"You all right, Mr. Stone?"

Was he? No and hell no he wasn't all right. He tried to shake off the uncomfortable shaft of desire that had him burning with a sudden need for the prickly woman. He'd had the most incredible vision of her wrapped around him as he pounded into her heat on the top of dark green counters.

Jared turned and looked at the man. "This is nothing like what I gave you to find for me and we both know it. If you take me to one more overpriced house you are trying to get rid of then I will find another realtor. Go over the list again and contact me when you have some that I will consider. I have neither the time nor the patience for this. Understand?" This was not how Jared wanted to spend his Friday night.

"Yes, sir. I'm sorry, sir. But the market has been—" Jared cut him off with a raised brow. "Of course," William went on. "I'll set you up for more of what you had in mind next week."

"This weekend if possible." Jared walked out the front door and got into his car. He'd had enough.

Monday morning he was going to confront the woman and tell her she was fired and to fire that Talbor. It was the surest way of getting her out of his system. And his dreams. That made him think of the dream he'd had of her last night, the one where he'd done all sorts of decadent things to the lovely Miss James. Slamming his hand against the steering wheel, he growled in frustration. And when he got home, he was calling every woman on his phone and exorcising Willow from his mind. He was frustrated, that was all. He needed to get laid. Somehow, as he pulled into his driveway, he knew that wasn't it at all.

~Chapter 5~

Willow was in the big office working when Thomas came and got her. He didn't say much, which wasn't anything unusual, but his facial expression said it all.

"He didn't mean to do it, boss. I think he being new and all…we can just fix it, right?"

She didn't say anything. New meant Robert and as much as she wanted to avoid the man altogether, she had to go and see what she could fix. If she could. The break room in the office building that she was led to didn't look all that bad at first glance. Then she saw what was going on.

The floor was to be tiled in white. No other colors were in the room, white walls, white counters and even white appliances, she'd been told. But there was a blue ribbon of tile all the way around the room a foot from any wall and six inches wide. And there in the corner about five feet from finishing was Robert.

"Fuck." She looked around the big room and tried to think.

She and Alexander had stayed up much too late talking last night. She hadn't even gone to bed when he'd left her house at three-thirty. She had a pounding headache and she was hungry because she'd skipped lunch again. It was just after three in the afternoon on a Friday and she was supposed to leave at five to pick up her brother and drive to Virginia with him.

"I read the wrong room. I didn't think to ask. I just saw the layout and laid the tile for the suite on the upper level. I'll pay for any changes." Jared didn't even look like he cared. In fact, if she was to guess, she'd say he was pissed...at her.

Willow pulled out her cell and punched in a few numbers. Well, she wasn't any happier with him either. That almost kiss had been driving her insane for a week now and she wanted him off her site. When the phone was answered, she had to do a quick change in temperament or this was going to put her behind.

"Hello, Snyder. It's Will James at the—"

"Ah my little builder, how is my building coming along? I went by there yesterday. It looks like you will be finished early."

Snyder Polson was the one and only Polson Enterprises— the man who was going to be moving into this building. He had been very specific on what he'd wanted and until today, she'd been following it to the tee.

"I fu...screwed up. Can you believe it? I was going along and laying that white tile we picked out and damned if I didn't add color in that lower break room. I'm so sorry. You have no idea how stupid I feel. I was nearly finished when one of my men came in and showed me my mistake." She closed her eyes when he didn't say anything.

She saw Thomas leave the room and felt Jared walk up beside her. She turned her back to him and was pissed when he moved into her view again. When she tried to turn again, he stayed her with his hands on her arms. She covered the mouth piece with her hand.

"This is so not the time to be fucking with me, Jared," Willow whispered to him. "Get out of my sight or so—"

"You were so close to being finished," Snyder said with a bit of astonishment in his voice. "Please tell me you can take it up. I think you know how much I dislike color in my eating areas."

She did, too. When they had had dinner a few months ago, she'd been amazed at the dining room in his house. The carpet, walls, table, and chairs had been a brilliant white. The flatware and even the plates had been the same non-color. When the food had arrived, she was surprised and pleased to see that it had color—absolutely no taste, but lots of color.

"I know. I know. It makes for a clean palate." She rolled her eyes when Jared grinned. "It will put me behind again…well, not behind, but not the two weeks early I was going for. I can't tell you how sorry I am for this, Snyder. We'll have to pull the flooring up and then reset the tile. The counters will have to be moved out again and—

"All that? You can't just, I don't know, just pull up the color? What color is it anyway? Please tell me it's not pink."

"No. Not pink. It's a dark royal blue. Pull up the color, you say? No, I wouldn't feel comfortable doing that. It would make the room off balanced and the tile wouldn't be lined up the way we discussed." She closed her eyes when Jared moved to her face.

He was listening, she knew, and he was close. And when the hell had he become Jared and not Robert? When she tried to draw away, he wrapped his arm around her waist and held her to him. Not really touching, but close enough. She felt her body respond to his scent and his warmth.

"I don't know, Will. I was looking forward to getting in there early. You know how much we're crammed into this building." She didn't point out that the one they were building was the same size. She could barely think. "And you say it's in the employee break room and not the executive one, correct?"

She had to swallow three times before she could answer. And she was positive that both men could hear her heart pounding in her chest. She nearly groaned out loud when Jared...Robert nuzzled her neck and placed an open mouthed kiss over her beating pulse.

~o0o~

"Answer him, Willow. He is giving you the okay." Jared's voice whispered in her ear, bringing his hot breath along the place on her neck where he'd kissed her.

"Yes. Yes, the employees' break room. I can't tell you again how...please don't." The last was a plea to Jared. He had pulled her body flush with his and she could feel his cock hard against her belly.

"Leave it, Willow. I think the employees might enjoy that bit of color to get out of this building and into a brand new one. Yes, color in there would be a wonderful idea. Thank you."

She didn't know if she answered Snyder, she wasn't even sure if she had hung up, but Jared's mouth over hers was suddenly all she could think about. And then she didn't think at all.

~o0o~

Her body fit to his. Her mouth was sex and heat and spice all in one. When she dropped the phone on his foot, he cupped her ass and brought her body flush with his. Her soft folds cupped his cock tightly. When her arms came up and encircled his neck, he lifted her higher and her legs wrapped around his hips. Jared was dizzy with need. Taking the two steps to the wall seemed an eternity and when he had her there, he wanted to toss her to the floor and take her on the dusty tile and cardboard boxes.

Cupping her breast, he felt the pearled tip strain against her bra. Willow wound her fingers in his hair and held him to her as he made his way down her jaw to her neck where her throat met her shoulder. Nipping at it gently, he pressed his cock against her and rocked hard. Her answering moan nearly undid him. Shifting, he pressed her tighter against the wall and held her up while he lifted her shirt with his now freed hands. The need to taste her hot flesh made him clumsy and he simply lifted her bra out of the way when he couldn't get the clasp undone.

"Please, please, I need you. I want you now. Please, Jared, I need—"

The voices in the hall outside the room froze them both in place. Neither of them moved. His mouth was a mere inch from her nipple and her fingers tangled in his hair. He wondered if he could lick her, take the morsel into his mouth just once. Would he have time to savor her taste? No, he realized when the voices in the hall seemed to be moving closer to them. Regret burning in his veins, he stepped back from the wall quickly and dropped her to the floor, her feet touching just as the men sounded around the corner. His cock was straining at the zipper, need making him ache. Looking at her now, he nearly snarled at the unseen men and went back to where they were.

Her cheeks were flushed red and her lips, full anyway, were swollen and pink. There was a burn along her jaw where his whiskers had scraped her and there was a small bite mark, bright red where he'd nipped her. She was panting; her breath was coming out in hot, short bursts. He turned away from her to adjust his cock when three men walked in with boxes of white tile and mortar.

"Hey, boss, you okay? You look like…well, I was gonna say like you was blushing, but that can't be so. You can tell a dirtier joke than me." Markus felt her forehead and then frowned. "You're hot too. You ain't coming down with something, are you? Bad time of year to get sick."

Jared felt a laughter bubble up. Yes, she certainly was hot. He could vouch for that. He started to turn back to her while he pulled his shirt out of his pants to try and hide his arousal, but he heard her moving out the door.

"The blue stays. I want this room finished before we leave tonight, guys. The appliances come on Monday and we need this ready." he turned to face her fully now and she wouldn't look at him. "Conley is in charge this weekend. If you guys have any issues, call him. I'm going to be out of town."

Markus laughed at her retreating back. "Like we don't know where she's going. Seen that man drop her off this morning? Nice-looking feller. Hope the boss gets her whistle wet. Might make her in a better mood."

The men moved off and Jared just stood there. It wasn't until Conley came back in that he realized he hadn't moved. He wasn't sure where he was going, but he suddenly needed to get out of the room. Leaving the building, he headed for the trailer and was stopped by a new SUV pulling in next to it.

A tall man with dark hair and a suit got out and was walking to the door when Willow came out and threw herself into his arms. Jared watched as he picked her up and swung her around then set her down with a kiss to her lips. To the lips he'd just kissed, the ones he'd tasted and bitten. With a growl of frustration, he started forward only to be stopped by Talbor.

"Didn't I tell you she was a slut? She got herself a rich one it looks like. We all wondered how she could afford that big house and all those improvements going on. Heard tell she was sleeping with the man who we're building this place for and that's how she got the job for old man Stone."

Jared turned and looked at Talbor. He knew the guy hated her. He didn't understand it, but he knew it. But she had just saved the company a great deal of money by sweet talking a man that Jared knew could be ruthless when things didn't go his way. Jared looked back at the vehicle as it pulled out of the lot. Willow James might not be sleeping with his dad, but she'd sure fallen into his arms quick enough. Going back into the building, he laid the rest of the tile.

He wasn't sure when he noticed that the men were giving him a wide berth, but he was glad for it. At seven o'clock, he punched out at the time clock and went to his truck. He had two houses to look at this weekend and then on Monday morning he was firing Will James. She was not going to suck him in.

~Chapter 6~

"I don't know why I did it, but Christ, it was hot." The drive to their parents' house was filled with short silences and a lot of changing the subjects.

Alexander knew something was wrong with his sister and wondered if it had anything to do with the man that had been glaring at them when he'd picked her up. That was a man who was pissed and it didn't take much to see why. He glanced over at Wills again and smiled at the dreamy look on her face and the bite mark on her throat that he knew hadn't been there this morning when she left.

They'd been talking about her recent trip to the Sahara Desert. She'd gone there with a group to see the vastness of it, she'd said, and to get some tile that she wanted for her house. The trip had been a success all the way around.

The tile in the kitchen was perfect. The rich dark green matched the countertops perfectly and the white and green tile on the floor in alternating blocks made the kitchen seem warm and cozy. Alexander chuckled softly when he thought of the time she'd put into a room she never used. Willow couldn't boil water without instructions and she would probably still screw it up.

"What's so funny?"

He looked over at his sister and smiled. "You are. Do you have any idea how beautiful you are? I'm betting you haven't put on a dress since last fall when Sheila got married."

She snorted. "If you remember correctly, I was the best man and I wore a tux. Why do you think I'm funny? Most people don't even like me."

He glanced over at her to see if she was kidding. It didn't appear that she was. Alexander was surprised she thought that. His vibrant, loving, and kind sister couldn't possibly be without friends. Taking a chance, he decided to go for broke. "What about that guy that was staring at us when we left? He looked like he wanted to murder me and then you."

She looked thoughtful. "Talbor? I don't doubt he wants me to keel over, but I don't think he gives two shits about you. I mean, do you know him?"

"Yes, I do. We went to school together. And it wasn't him. Tall guy, light hair, intense, maybe a little pissed. The one who put the hickey on your neck."

Her hand went to her throat quickly. Then she pulled down the visor to have a look in the mirror. When she sat back and groaned, he knew he'd hit the mark. She looked out the window before she answered.

"He works for me. He...we kissed and it...we might have...I might have let it go too far. It can't happen again." She glanced at him when he did her and their eyes caught. "How did you know?"

Alexander looked back at the road. His sister was very smart, brilliant as a matter of fact. But she was incredibly naive about the opposite sex. He glanced back at her and wondered, not for the first time, if she was still a virgin.

She'd gone through high school and college when most kids her age were discovering themselves. Willow had been discovering everything—as long as it was in a book or a class. By the time he'd gotten his first job in the computer world, Willow was working full time as a gopher on a job site. When Alexander was dating and having sex with any woman that was willing, Willow was working her way through a business degree. He doubted she'd had that much fun as a teenager. And now at twenty-six, she was just as inexperienced as most kids half her age.

"He looked like he was ready to tear me apart for touching you, that's how I know. How long has this been going on?"

Willow didn't say anything for a while. He was sure she wasn't going to answer him. "He started working for me a couple of weeks ago. And you have to be wrong about the touching me thing. He and I only kissed today and nothing before then. He's too…you're just wrong about it."

Alexander wondered about the "he's too" for the rest of the ride home because she had snuggled down in the seat and closed her eyes. It was something she'd done as a child when she didn't want to talk about something. Hide out until the other party gave up or something else came up. He decided to talk to their mom. She would know how to handle it.

It was nearly midnight when he got the chance to talk to his mom. But she'd already figured out something was wrong and had cornered him in the kitchen when he'd gone in for another piece of cherry pie after dinner. His mother, Amanda James, was as subtle as a bull in a china house.

"What's wrong with Wills? And who is she sleeping with?" Alexander had a mouth full of pie and she'd startled him into just staring at her.

He took his time chewing then swallowing. He didn't want his sister to be pissed at him. She had a wicked temper. It was quick to ignite and quicker to burn out. But she was vicious when she was at full throttle. Just like their mother.

"She didn't tell me his name, but I gathered he works for her. They aren't sleeping together, but that might change soon if his looks were any indication. Why?"

Amanda sat down and looked at him. She was grinning. He decided he didn't like that grin and started to leave the kitchen before she brought him into whatever she was thinking.

"Oh no you don't, young man. Get back in here right now. Sit." Alexander sat. His mom was still his mom and he was slightly…okay, he was terrified of her. "Spill it. And don't leave out anything."

So he did. He didn't really know much. The bite mark appearing on her neck, the way she said it couldn't happen again. And he had to describe the man once for her and then again for his dad. Alexander was sure that when Wills found out, and he didn't doubt she would, he was a dead man.

~o0o~

Willow got up early the next morning and went to the kitchen. She loved the mornings and was thrilled that Shasta had made her sticky buns for breakfast. This made life all the more worth it. Hot buns and a glass of iced tea.

"You eat all them Missy Wills. You don't eat enough for a bird. I think you lost more weight since I seen you last. I'm going to tell that girl of mine she needs to feed you more."

She was probably right. Willow was eating her third bun when her dad came into the kitchen. They had been sharing breakfast since she was a child. She didn't realize how much she missed it until just then.

"You save any for me?" Edgar James got a cup of coffee, kissed Shasta on the cheek, and sat down at the table. "So, girl, tell me who's been sucking on your neck."

Willow snorted tea up her nose and nearly choked to death on the bun lodged in her throat. While Shasta beat her back hard enough to break ribs, her dad sat across from her laughing. She was going to kill Alexander.

"What the heck, dad? Sucking on my neck? I do work on a construction site. It's a…it's a bruise." Shasta snickered; her dad laughed harder.

"You're a terrible liar and you always have been. Now, tell me, little girl, do I need a shotgun here or are you telling me you've been practicing safe sex?" he sat back in his chair. "I gotta tell you, I'm hoping for both right now. Nothing on this earth would make me happier than you having your own baby. But I'd prefer you did it the right way. You know, married then baby. Right now…well, I wouldn't even care if it was less than nine months from bride to mother."

Willow looked at her dad, really looked. He was her best friend, always had been. She really was a terrible liar, but she thought that was more because she hated to lie to the one man she would love forever.

"It's not like that. It was a kiss that I let get away from me. It should—"

Her dad suddenly sat up in his chair. "Did he force you, baby girl? I'll kill the son of a bitch. Alexander didn't say…"

"Oh no, don't stop now. What did my brother, who I might add isn't long for this earth, have to say to you? Damn it all to hell in a hand basket." She stood up to find her brother. "Is he still here?"

"Now Wills, don't hurt him. He was just concerned, that's all." her dad started edging toward the door as he spoke. Whether to stop her or to warn Alexander, she didn't know. But her brother chose that moment to step through the door.

She lunged for him as her dad tried to push Alexander back. Willow was quicker and caught him around the neck before he could get away. Her dad didn't move quickly enough and went down when she and Alexander did. She cuffed her brother in the mouth. There were a few stray punches, some to her and some she landed. She was just straddling her brother's chest to drop his head on the tile floor a few times when ice cold water hit her in the face.

"Mother fuck!" Willow tried to get away from the spray, but it seemed to be following her everywhere. She moved off Alexander only to have the water follow her there too. She opened her mouth to scream at someone and heard her mother's voice. The "you are so fucked" voice.

"One more, Willow Dawn James, one more cuss word and you will eat an entire bar of soap. Alexander Patterson James, get up from that floor this minute. And you." She snapped at her husband of thirty-five years. "You are well grown and should know better."

"Me?" her dad asked incredulously. "I was trying to keep her from hurting her brother."

A single raising of her hand had the three of them shutting up. Willow wanted to kick out at her brother, but her mother simply looked at her and she drew her foot back to her body.

"Who started this?"

Willow opened her mouth to say Alexander had when her brother beat her to it, blaming her for the whole thing.

"I was coming in for breakfast when Wills attacked—"

"I most certainly did not," she snapped at him. "You, you big-mouthed as…wiener head had to blab about my hickey. Why couldn't you just—"

"I didn't say anything until Mom cornered me in the kitchen last night. And if you ask me, it's about time you get laid. You must be the oldest living virgin on the planet."

Pain ripped through her heart as silence blanketed the room. Her mouth hurt and so did her jaw. She was soaking wet sitting on the cold floor and none of that mattered as much as the embarrassment and humiliation she felt. They knew, all of them knew. She stood up and so did her father. She couldn't look at any of them.

"Honey," her dad started. "Don't, baby. He didn't mean to—"

She brushed past him with a mumbled "excuse me," left the kitchen, and went up to her room quickly.

She heard Alexander shouting for her, her mom too. But she didn't slow down. When she got to her room and locked the door, she let the tears fall. She went to her bathroom and with that door closed and locked too, she crawled into the tub and let go.

Even over her sobs, she could hear someone at the door. Her cell phone went off twice in rapid succession, but she wasn't in the mood to speak to them just yet. Willow wasn't really mad at them...well, maybe her brother, but she knew she wouldn't stay that way for long.

This wasn't the first time their mother had hosed them down to get them to stop fighting. But it was the first time in the house. Willow grinned when she thought about the look on Shasta's face. Willow and Alexander were always fighting as kids. They never stayed angry with each other. But if either of them needed help with a bully or even another kid, they'd be the first to stand up.

Willow was embarrassed that her family knew she was still a virgin. Leaning her head back against the tub wall, she wondered if she was a freak or something. She knew that her brother was a ladies' man; hell, the entire campus where they had both gone to college had known that. But little Wills James was too young and then too smart to be considered anything but a nerd.

Climbing out of the bath an hour later, Willow looked at herself in the mirror. There was a bruise on her jaw forming and her nose had been bleeding. Turning on the taps at the sink, she tugged the rubber band out of her messy braid and pulled out a comb. The water was ice cold by then so she washed her face of the blood and tears. While she tried to get her hair back under some sort of order, she closed her eyes and thought about Jared.

No one had ever made her lose control like he had. She had always been the one to stop men from getting past kissing her. With Jared…Robert, she hadn't wanted him to. In fact, it had been everything she could do not to order the men out of the building and have him take her against the hard floor, or the wall, or the window. And his hands…she knew they'd feel good against her skin and couldn't wait until next time. Her eyes popped open.

Staring at her reflection, she pointed at herself. "No next time. This can't happen again. He works for you. Enough people already think you slept your way to where you are. Behave." With that, she straightened up and went to her room.

Stripping down, she went to her closet to get some dry clothes. She knew that she was leaving tonight and decided to get something soft on now for the drive. Alexander was staying on for a few days before heading back to his home in Cincinnati. She was making the return three hour trip by herself and wanted to be comfy for the drive. When she opened her door, her brother was sitting on the floor across from her room with his back to the wall behind him.

She walked over, sat on the floor next to him, and leaned her head on his shoulder. "I'm sorry I hit you."

"I'm sorry I embarrassed you. I shouldn't have said that to you." She felt the tears well up again as he kissed her head.

They sat that way for a while then went back downstairs. No one mentioned the incident and the water had been cleaned up. Willow kissed her father's fat lip and told him she was sorry. Her mother held her tight then they all went to the pumpkin patch to buy their Halloween decoration for beggar's night, which was in ten days.

~*Chapter 7*~

Jared was drunk. He knew this because he'd wanted to get that way and had worked his way through all of Saturday night getting there. It hadn't been as hard as it used to be, but he was quite happy with the results.

He'd been pissed about something, but had completely forgotten what it was by his eighth beer…or was it his ninth? He grinned sloppily when he thought of the woman he'd brought home with him. He turned to look at her. He frowned when he couldn't find her.

"Willow?" He looked under the cushions on the couch. "You got some explaining to do."

He laughed like a loon when he realized what he'd said then forgot what was so funny, and that made him laugh harder. He continued his search of the girl and her name.

"Not William…Willow. Nah, not that either. Come out, come out…pistol? No that's not it." He looked under the coffee table and got distracted by the reflection of himself in the glass. He was making faces at himself when something occurred to him.

"Who would name their little girl after a gun? Smith and Wesson?" he shushed himself when he realized he had been talking really loud. "Course who'd thunk to name their kid after a tree? Willow? Where are you?"

Beard came into the room when Jared came out from behind the couch. He laughed again when he had startled the man.

"Sir, are you all right? You seem to be...well, inebriated."

Jared nodded at the man, but had to stop when it made him dizzy. "Nope. Drunk. Drunk as a skunk." Jared frowned. "Do skunks get drunk as a skunk when they drunk...drink? Beard, did you see my tree? I can't seem to find her."

Jared dropped behind a chair, sure something had moved. He lay down for a minute while the room took a turn. He closed his eyes and that made it worse. When he opened them again, there stood Beard.

"Tree, sir? I don't understand. You came home in that cab alone an hour ago. No one else has come in since. Were you expecting someone?" Beard helped him to his feet—all six of them. He was thinking with that many feet, he should be able to stand straighter.

"I think I should lie down. Here is good." They were on the stairs then and Jared looked behind him to see how they'd gotten that far. Magic, he thought.

"Very good, sir. If you'll just stop—oof. Sir, you must refrain from stomping my feet. It is quite painful." Jared staggered his way up to his bedroom, or really, Beard had half-dragged half-carried him up to his room.

When Jared hit the bed, his entire body felt like it had been twisted in a tight wad and then run over. He lurched up and stumbled to the bathroom and threw up. Throwing up sobered a person quickly, he discovered, but he felt like shit afterwards. Jared didn't know how he got into his bed, but he was suddenly there and his legs were being tugged off. Looking down, he saw that Beard was pulling off his shoes. He was glad for that. He needed them.

"Beard? I'm pretty sure I'm going to want you to shoot me in the morning. Why don't you just do it now and save you the trouble?"

"No, sir. I'm afraid that's quite impossible. You've gone to a great deal of trouble to get in this state and I think you should suffer through it until the end." The light went off as Beard continued. "Besides, sir, it would be a ghastly mess and I don't want to have to explain to the lady of the house how you came to be dead on my watch."

Jared was closing his eyes when he realized that Beard had made a joke. Raising his head, he looked toward the door. He hoped it was a joke anyway. Jared was out before his head hit the pillow the second time.

His head was broken. Jared had been trying to get up for over an hour and couldn't get his head to work. Sometime after leaving the bar—or was it bars?—he'd done something to break his head. Rolling to his back only made it worst. Closing his eyes again, he sat up slowly and when the room stopped spinning, Jared staggered to the bathroom.

There was aspirin and a glass of orange juice sitting on the counter along with a bottle of beer and a glass. The note tied around the bottle of beer simply said, "hair of the dog." Jared's belly rebelled at the thought of putting any more alcohol in his system. But he did take six of the aspirin and drained the glass of juice. Turning on the shower, he waited for the water to get hot and looked at himself in the mirror.

He looked like shit, and that, he decided, was an understatement. His eyes were bloodshot and his nose was bright red. His lip was bleeding and a little puffy, but he didn't have a clue what he'd done. His tongue felt like he had a hairy rug on it and when he opened his mouth to see if his teeth had individual sweaters on them, he discovered they were just teeth. He brushed his teeth four times before he felt like they were clean.

His chest ached and he remembered throwing up. Then he remembered Beard helping him up the stairs. Jared sat down on the toilet when everything from last night came into focus with perfect clarity. Everything.

Willow. This was all her fault. She'd led him on and now...well, he didn't really need all that much leading. He stood up and shucked his clothes as he remembered touching her, kissing her. Christ, he wanted her.

Jared stepped into the shower and nearly killed himself trying to turn the water to warm. Someone had turned the taps all the way to cold. He didn't want to think it was the man who'd left him the juice and hairy dog this morning. Adjusting the water, he scrubbed his skin and his thoughts once again drifted to Willow.

She had let him touch her when she had someone else in her life. He didn't like to think about the fact that if she let Jared do the things he'd done to her, what would she let the man in the parking lot do to her? He wouldn't have a woman he couldn't trust in his life, not again. He'd had one too many over the years, women who wanted money and a good name to go with it. Jared wondered what she wanted.

Jared was dressing when he thought about her and Conley together. He had no doubt now that she was having an affair with Conley, a married man. That bothered him too because he knew from his file that Conley had three kids. What sort of woman had an affair with a married man with kids? Then on top of that, would two-time him with Jared. He made his way down the stairs to the kitchen.

Beard was there with one of the maids, Jared had no idea who, telling her about the linens in the front bedroom. She scurried away when she saw him. Jared watched the door swing back and forth after she'd gone until Beard cleared his throat.

"Sir. How are you feeling this afternoon?" Jared looked up at the clock. It was just after three in the afternoon.

"Fine. No, shitty. I'm really sorry about last night. I was a complete ass and I can't tell you how stupid I feel."

Beard nodded. Jared wasn't sure if he was accepting the apology or agreeing with his assessment of him being an ass. He decided that maybe he didn't want to know. Beard asked him if he was hungry.

The thought of food made his belly jump. "No, I don't think I'll ever eat again. Or drink. I think I've hit my limit for the rest of my life."

Jared pulled a mug from the cabinet and poured himself some coffee. It was fresh and hot. Nothing like the tar they served at the site. He wondered if Willow would be working today and decided he'd drive by and see. He was still going to fire her in the morning, but did want to see if she was working. He told Beard not to make dinner for him, that he'd get something in town. He was pulling out of the gated drive twenty minutes later.

Before he knew it, he was in the lot and his truck was off. The same beat up pickup was sitting there and there were lights on inside the building and the site trailer. He got out of the truck and walked to the office. He didn't really want to talk to her, but wanted to make sure she wasn't in there with Conley.

~o0o~

Willow was working her way through the invoices when someone knocked. Since the door was never locked when she was there, she yelled for whoever it was to come in. Jared came in and slammed the door back on its hinges.

"Do you have any idea what I could have done to you if I had wanted to? That fucking door should be locked when you're here alone." He made a big deal out of turning the tab. "Where's Conley?"

She glanced up at him, but didn't want to get into a fight with him so she answered his question. Fucking bastard, she so didn't need this shit today.

"Home. Where you should be. Go away, I'm busy." She screamed when her chair was jerked away from the desk and turned to him. "Are you fucking nuts? Get out of here."

He loomed over her. Close, so close she could see each individual lash on his eyes. And his breath blew in soft puffs over her mouth. But it was his eyes that threw her. They were deeper, darker than they had been before.

Need, unfamiliar and powerful, coiled inside of her. But before she could do something stupid like pull him down to her mouth for a quick nibble—or a long one—he wrenched away from her and crossed to the other side of the desk.

Willow moved slowly back to the desk, not sure what would set him off again. Picking up the next invoice, she laid it back down because she didn't want him to see how hard her hands were shaking.

"You've driven me insane all weekend," he said softly as he flopped down in the only other chair in the trailer. "I even got drunk so I could try and get you out of my mind."

Willow wondered if there was a sign hanging on her somewhere that said, "rip out my heart, I don't need it." She tried to mask her hurt by looking down at the now blurry paper in front of her.

"How did that work out for you?" She heard him chuckle, but didn't look up from the computer. "The men in my life just use a punching bag."

He didn't say anything for a long time, so long that she looked back at him. She was uncomfortable under his scrutiny and nearly asked him to please go away again. But his next words sliced through her.

"Just how many men are in your life, Willow? I mean, besides the man from the other day, Conley, and any number of men who work for you." he sifted in the chair. "I mean, there are what...twenty-five men on this crew give or take?"

Willow stood up and walked to the door. She was leaving, she had to. And she didn't care what he thought about it. She had just had enough. Then suddenly, she was pressed against the door, Jared's breath, his body, on hers.

"All of them. All the men that work for me now and in the past are men in my life." her voice cracked, but she wanted him to leave her alone. "It's really too bad I don't have an opening right now or I'd slip you in."

When he didn't move, didn't back away, she tried to push back and to make him move, but he simply held her there.

"Let me go. I mean it. I want you to let me go." She felt him back up and she took a deep breath, hoping that she would make it to her truck before the tears fell. But he turned her around so that her back was now pressed against the door and him against her.

"I can't. I wish that I could, but I simply can't." His cock pressed hard into her and she felt her body respond to him. "Let me have you, Willow. Even for this one night. Let me bury myself inside of you."

Taking a deep breath, she turned in his embrace and pushed him back. He moved, but didn't let her go. She looked up into his eyes and saw lust, passion, and need burning in them. She wondered fleetingly if her own eyes said the same thing.

Willow knew without a doubt that it was going to be a mistake, but she wanted him. There would be this one night, she promised herself, then it would be finished. She wasn't worried about his noticing she was a virgin and if he did figure it out…well, then it would be too late anyway.

"Tonight. Only tonight and then you stay away from me." When he nodded, she thought of his accusations. "And no questions. Ever. We have sex then you and I are never again. I'll meet you at the hotel on Broad Street."

He stepped back from her. "Do you get a discount there, Willow?" Hurt and pain seared through her being, but she refused to show him.

"Do you want this or not? Frankly, I could care less," she snarled at him.

He hesitated just long enough that she thought he was going to tell her no. She wasn't sure in that moment if she would be happy or not about it. But he nodded again.

"Yes, damn you, I want you. I'll meet you there. I need to get me some protection first." he wrapped his hand around the back of her neck and jerked her to him. This kiss was brutal, almost savage. When he pulled away, she was breathless and wanted him more now than she had before.

"But this one night is mine, all mine, Willow. No other thought but me in that pretty little head of yours. You understand me?"

She nodded to him this time, not sure if opening her mouth would be safe. She didn't know what sort of nonsense would spill from her lips. Turning, she left the trailer.

Walking to her truck, she had to concentrate on putting one foot in front of the other. Her knees were wobbly and she was sure there would be burn on her skin where he had touched her.

Stopping at the front desk at the cheap hotel on Broad, she had to stop the uncontrollable urge to laugh. Jared had asked her if she got a discount at this hotel when, in fact, she'd never paid for one in all her life. She'd never had too.

The James family, her father actually, owned several hotels, The James Suites, all over the world. She had never thought about the fact that they'd never paid. Since they owned them, it would be pointless. But they had been taught at a very young age to tip and to tip well. Willow's family had been in the hotel business for four generations and she would be the fifth when she was ready. Her brother Alexander had already told their father that he had no interest in them.

Taking the key from the clerk, she made her way to room seventeen. She wasn't sure how Jared would know where she was staying, but went inside and closed the door. She nearly turned and left again when she got a good look at the room.

The bed was a full and took up most of the space in the smallish room. It was covered with the most hideous comforter she'd ever seen. It was pink, purple, and green paisley print that looked as if it had been painted by a three-year-old. And not only did the print cover the bed, but the curtains as well. And if Willow wasn't mistaken, she thought she could see it in the bathroom too.

The carpet was brown. There was no other way to describe it other than to say it was muddy brown, and even that she was sure wasn't just a color, but actual mud. It had probably been shag at some point, but now it was just nappy.

There was an end table on either side of the bed with a lamp screwed to the top of both of them. A remote on a cable, also attached to the table, was lying there as well. The only other piece of furniture besides the television was a dresser. It was beat up and one of the pulls was missing. Going into the bathroom, she could see the "style," if one could call it that, extended into here as well.

The shower curtain was the same paisley puke color as the one in the bedroom, but in here the decorator had really gone all out. A pink commode graced the center of the far wall and a green counter top had a coffee maker and an ice bucket with one plastic glass wrapped in plastic. These both sat on a bright yellow tray. The tub, a startling shade of purple, was directly across from the sink. It would have been funny if she wasn't so depressed.

Since Willow had no clue how any of this was supposed to work, she went out to her truck and got her bag from when she'd left her parents' house. Jared was just pulling up when she closed up her truck. He raised his brow at her case, but wisely kept his mouth shut. She handed him one of the keys and followed him inside.

If he had an opinion about the room, he didn't say. She looked around the room and realized that it hadn't improved in the ten minutes she'd been gone. Shifting her bag over her shoulder, she turned to him and that's when she saw the bag in his hands.

Condoms. He'd said he was picking them up. Trying hard not to look at the bag or the man, she moved to the bathroom door. She knew she was escaping, but right now, she needed a minute to think.

~Chapter 8~

Jared waited until the door shut behind her before he sat down and took his first real breath since he'd left the site trailer. He looked down at the box of condoms in his fingers and wondered, not for the first time, what the fuck he was doing.

He'd been standing at the display of condoms reading the labels when he read the tag line, "for her pleasure." Willow's pleasure. Then he began to get slightly panicky when he realized she might have more experience than him at having one night stands. Not that he had many, but she was a walking advertisement for sex. He looked around the room and laughed. He wondered if she spent a lot of time in these rooms and decided that he didn't want to know. Jared stood up, tossed the box on the bed, and started unbuttoning his shirt.

There wasn't any reason to pretend that they were there for any other reason than to fuck each other. And he had told her all night so she was clear it wasn't going to be a "wham, bam, thank you, ma'am" kind of fuck either. He wanted her out of his system once and for all. Then after Monday when she was gone, he could go about his business.

He glanced up at the bathroom door when he heard the shower turn on. He smiled and thought they might as well get started right now.

The door opened easily and then steam hit him hard. A soft scent of lavender filled his nose and he smiled at how much that smell suited her. He could see her bare arms as she raised her hands up, and need hit him hard in the gut. He quickly finished undressing.

Fisting the two packages in his hand, Jared slipped into the shower, pulling the curtain back into place as the water hit him. She stood under the spray rinsing the soap from her hair and Jared got his first look at perfection.

Her hair hung in a long coil of silk down her back to just her hips. Her legs looked muscled, well-toned, and long. He could almost feel them wrapped around his body. When she turned around, she jumped slightly, but all that did was draw his attention to her breasts. They were full and heavy, her nipples hard and a dark pink. His mouth watered at the memory of nearly getting to taste one and wondered if she would allow him to suckle them as he fucked her. At her sharp intake of breath, he looked to her face.

She was staring at his cock and he felt it lengthen and harden more at her gaze. He watched her face as he fisted his cock, moving his hand up and down to see what she would do. He moaned when she licked her lips and groaned. He had all night with her and wondered for a second if all his life would be enough.

"I want you. I will have you all night as we agreed, right?" She looked up at his face now and Jared thought he saw fear, but it was there and gone so quickly that he was sure he'd been mistaken.

Taking a step toward her, he watched as she straightened up. Reaching above his head, Jared laid the two condoms on the ledge and took her mouth.

She was slick and hot. Her body slid over his as he pressed her back against the wall. The sensation of her touching him fully made him moan again. When her hands came up and encircled his neck, Jared lifted her breasts up from beneath and ran the pads of his thumbs over each nipple. Releasing her mouth, he leaned down, took her left nipple into his mouth, and swirled his tongue around the tight peak before he suckled hard on it.

Her fingers lacing into his hair held him to her as he ate at her breast. Switching back and forth, Jared sampled each one until he needed more from her, wanted more of her. When he pulled back, she whimpered and he nearly took her again. But it was the soft curls between her thighs that beckoned him now. He needed to taste all of her and would if it was the last thing he did.

Dropping to his knees, Jared gently touched her ankles and pressed against them to have her widen her legs. Then, running his fingers up and down her calves, he kissed the area just above her pussy. Then he moved his mouth to her hips, first one then the other as he nipped her then kissed it gently to take away the hurt. He looked up at her from his position on the floor.

Her eyes were hooded and her lips swollen. Jared had never in all his life seen a more beautiful sight than her at that moment. And never had he wanted anyone as much as he did this woman. Trailing his fingers up her thigh then down the other side, he reached up and danced his tongue in her belly button before he spoke.

"Willow, I'm going to take you into my mouth. I'm going to sip from your nectar, then I'm going to take you hard against this wall. Then when we're done in here, I'm going to take you to that ugly bed and start all over again." As he leaned forward to take her, she stayed him with her hand.

"Jared, you said one night. Never again after this. You understand, right?"

Jared felt anger surge through his body. How dare she? How dare she set rules up when she slept with every man she could. He leaned forward again and slid three of his fingers deep into her heat as he suckled her clit into his mouth.

~oOo~

Willow wanted to scream when he took her. She felt every stroke of his tongue, as he worried her clitoris. His fingers moved in and out of her, stretching her and filling her. She wanted to beg him for his cock, beg him to take her now and not later, but she could barely breathe. She didn't think she could speak too.

A slight movement, a deeper push inside of her, and a nip at her clit brought her over the edge. Her body felt suspended for several seconds, as if it didn't know what to do, then it plunged over the top. Every part of her body felt the release. Even as her body was coming down, but still simmering at a low burn, Jared continued to assault her senses until she came again then a third time.

Grabbing his head, she pulled him away. Her knees trembled and her legs felt like jelly. She was sure that they weren't going to hold her up and braced her free hand against the wall behind her. Heart pounding, she looked down at him.

"Please, no more. I beg you, please. I can't do it again. You've drained me." He stood up and crushed her mouth beneath his.

Willow had been kissed before, plenty of times. But this man could and did take her breath away. His tongue held her taste, spicy and hot, erotic and sweet. She rolled her own along his, suddenly energized, suddenly ready for more. When his cock nudged at her soft folds, Willow reached between them and wrapped her fingers around him.

His cock was both soft and hard and thick in her hand. Running her fisted hand up and down the shaft to the tip, she felt him jerk. Jared then surged against her as he tore her mouth from hers.

"Baby, you keep that up and I'm going to come all over you." Willow looked down and wondered how that would feel, but before she could ask or continue her journey, he handed her a condom.

"Please, Willow. I can't wait any longer to be inside of you. I need to fuck you now."

Her fingers felt clumsy and she bobbled the package twice before she could see how to open it. Brushing his cock with her hand when she had to capture the condom again, he groaned and fell back against the wall, turning off the water.

His body glistened with droplets of water. His hair hung down his back in a curtain of wet silk. Willow liked looking at him and wondered what he would do if she touched him. Forgetting about the condom for now, she took a step toward him and touched.

The muscles around his nipples rippled when she ran her fingers around the dark brown caps. His nipples peaked and hardened immediately. Reaching up with her other hand, she rolled them both in between her fingers until they were rock hard and begging her to taste. Giving into temptation, she nipped one gently with her teeth and his answering groan made her feel bold. Moving closer to his chest and much like he had her, Willow sampled him. First one then the other nipple.

"Willow, honey," he begged her hoarsely. "Please, you're killing me. I'm not going to last much longer and I want to be inside of you."

His voice, dark with need, made her body respond. She felt her pussy gush her cream and she nearly cried out when he cupped her breast again and took her nipple in his mouth. Opening the condom, she took it out and touched it to the tip of his cock.

Jared stayed her hands with his bigger ones and pulled them away. He took the condom from her. Looking at his face, he looked to be in pain and his mouth was a tight line. She wanted to smooth out the frown and kiss away the tightness, but he scooped her up in his arms and carried her to the bedroom.

When they were beside the bed, he cupped her cheeks in his hands and kissed her. This kiss was gentle, soft, and sweet. He nipped at her lips before tilting her head slightly and taking the kiss deeper. Her head moved to the side and he began to devour her mouth as he lifted her breasts. When he let go and stepped back, he nodded to the bed.

"Lie down. Please. If I continue to touch you without being inside of you, I'm going to be finished before we've begun. Next time, Willow. Next time I'll take my time with you. I promise. But for now, I'm too close. Lie down and let me fuck you."

Hurt like slow burn touched her again. Not at him but at herself. How could she have let herself forget what this way about? This was just sex, an itch to scratch. Something he wanted to do to exorcise her from his thoughts. Turning toward the bed to hide her anger, he stopped her with a hand to her arm.

"What is it? What's wrong?" She must have looked as confused as she felt; surely he didn't know what she was thinking. "It's only to get this out of our systems, Willow. You're the one who keeps saying it's only for tonight. And it will have to be regardless. I don't share when I'm with a woman."

Anger made her words come out uncensored. "Fuck you, Jared. I'm not with anyone. What makes you so sure that this will work? Huh? You think so little of me, or is it you? Do you think you're that fucking good? Fine."

She threw herself on the bed and spread her thighs open wide. She knew what she must look like and didn't care.

"Go ahead. Fuck me out of your system, as you said. I'm about finished here anyway. Let's get this over with."

He had the condom on in seconds and dropped his weight onto her. She was sure she should be afraid, maybe even terrified, but she wasn't. He was going to take her and she couldn't wait to feel him. But he was angry like her and when he plunged into her in one hard stroke, she screamed out her pain then bit her lip until she tasted blood.

"Christ," he hissed and started to roll off her, but she couldn't let him to do that. There would be questions, more than she wanted to answer, and she wrapped her legs around his hips.

The burning pain was quick to dissipate, the pain short lived. When she turned her head away from his prying eyes, she rolled her hips to make herself more comfortable. Incredible pleasure raced up her core. Moving again had Jared rock into her. Adjusting her legs, she felt him press deeper, harder until she was sure she couldn't take anymore of him.

He tried several times to move her head back, but she didn't want him to see her tears and she didn't want to see his face. She was sure that he was going to be disappointed and only hoped that he didn't tell anyone what she had been.

When she rolled her hips beneath him, she felt the now familiar tightening begin to build.

Moving upward with each of his stokes down, they set a tentative rhythm until she got the hang of it. A climax was building quicker now and she reached for it even as she tried to give him as much pleasure as she knew how.

Then Jared hit something inside of her, a spot, and she knew suddenly that it was her sweet spot. She'd heard girls in college talk about it all the time and he'd found hers. Every time he brushed against it, she felt her climax rising to the surface. And when it hit, she went screaming.

It ripped from her and destroyed her. Before she was coming back to earth again, she came again, then again. She couldn't breathe, couldn't think. When Jared surged into her deeper and harder, throwing back his head and shouting, Willow came again and slipped into a dark place.

~Chapter 9~

Jared dropped onto Willow again. This time he wasn't pissed, but because of pure exhaustion. He raised his head slightly, about all he could manage, and looked down at her. She was asleep or out, and for some odd reason, that pleased him that he had rendered her unconscious. Using what little strength he had, he turned her face toward his with a finger to her cheek.

Tears still rolled down her cheeks and blood was on her lip. Jared captured a tear on his finger as he said her name softly. She didn't stir. Rolling to his side, he lay there on his back, looked up at the water stain on the ceiling, and tried to figure out what the hell he had just done.

Before he could do anything that would hurt her more, he got up and went to the bathroom to flush the condom and noticed the streaks of blood on it and his leg. He sat down hard on the side of the tub and felt a wave of dizziness wash over him. A virgin. Willow was…no, she had been a virgin.

Jared stood again, leaned on the ugly counter, and looked at the stranger reflected back at him. He decided that he didn't like that man all that much. In fact, he was pretty sure he could hate him. The man in the mirror seemed to be saying, "She should have told you. It's not your fault," but Jared knew that it was.

He had wanted her and went after her, refusing to see anything else but the picture someone else had painted of her. He was as bad, if not worse, than Talbor. Jared turned off the light and went into the bedroom to find Willow awake and talking on the phone with a sheet wrapped around her. When he sat on the edge of the bed, she turned away from him as she continued her call.

"Yes, please…Yes, I'll…wait. Can you wait just one second? Thanks." She put her hand over the receiver and looked over her shoulder toward him, but not at him. "I'm ordering a pizza. Would you like something other than Coke and a large meaty one?"

He reached out to her and she moved away from his touch. "Willow, look at me. Please?" She turned her back to him again and huffed.

"Do you want anything to eat or not? I'm sure they want to close up sometime tonight."

Jared glanced down at his watch and saw it was only seven o'clock. He doubted that was an issue, but didn't say anything. He decided to wait until later to talk to her about what they had done.

"That sounds good. Whatever you're having is fine."

He got up as she told the person on the phone to double her order. He was slipping on his underwear when he heard the phone click closed. He turned and looked at her.

"Are you all right, Willow?" She mumbled something back and he was reasonably sure he didn't want her to repeat it. But he was angry now and wanted her to speak to him or at least look at him.

"Willow, look at me, damn it. Did I hurt you?"

She turned then and scooted herself up to the headboard. She adjusted the sheet several times, enough times that he wanted to jerk it off her and make her stop it. She looked up at him before she spoke.

"I'm fine. Just peachy, as a matter of fact. You know, we have about twenty-five minutes before the food arrives. Wanna have another go around?" The sheet ripped away. "You still have eleven condoms left and I want you to get your money's worth."

Jared was tempted to shuck his pants again and do just what she had suggested. But he already hated himself and was sure if he gave into his baser needs, he'd never forgive himself. Leaning over, he picked up the discarded sheet, intending to cover her back up with it.

"We need to talk, Willow. We have to talk about—"

He nearly fell over when she started cupping her breasts and tugging at her nipples. The sheet he'd picked up was now forgotten in his fingers.

"I didn't realize that my nipples were so sensitive before. You rolling them in your mouth was wonderful." She sat up on the bed and threw back her head as she continued to drive him over the edge. "Would you like to do that again, Jared?"

Willow didn't wait for his answer, not that he could talk around his tongue hanging out, but when she sat on the edge of the bed with him between her legs, he took a step forward and his shins touched her knees.

Jared watched her play and the darker pink her nipples got, the harder he did. His cock ached now. And the way he felt, he'd never know that he he'd just had the most incredible climax of his life not twenty minutes before. But when she lifted her left breast up and licked her nipple, Jared felt his eyes roll to the back of his head as she moaned her pleasure.

Christ, she was killing him. He watched mesmerized as his hand reached out and cupped the back of her head. But instead of bringing her to her feet as he wanted, she leaned in and rubbed her cheek against his cloth-covered cock.

He would never know how it happened, never remember how one second he was standing next to the bed with her face on his cock and the next lying on the bed, his shorts off and Willow on the floor between his thighs. Leaning up on his elbows, Jared looked down at her as she slid her hands up his thighs. His cock danced and bobbed on his belly, waiting for her next move.

"Touch me like before. Wrap your hand around me and hold me, Willow." her grip was firm, but not painful. "That's it, baby. Now slide your hand up and down. Up over my head and…shit. Willow, that's it!"

Her hands heated his already hot flesh. When he felt her other hand cup his balls and roll them, he couldn't help the strangled cry that erupted from his mouth. She jerked back as though she were scalded.

"Baby, you." He had to clear his throat twice before he continued. "You didn't hurt me. Christ, you can't believe how good you feel. Please don't stop. I'm beg—"

Her mouth covered him, his cock jumped, and he nearly came then. Lying back on the bed, it was all he could do not to beg her to never stop. But he sat up again because he needed to watch her. Cupping her head, he showed her, guided her up and down his shaft and when her tongue curled around his engorged head, he surged up into her mouth and touched the back of her throat. When she adjusted her body to fit closer to his, he felt her breast brush against his balls and knew that he was a goner. He thought if she was this good as a novice, she was going to kill him when she got a bit more practice.

Now he held her as he surged into her. He knew that it was only a matter of seconds now and he was going to come. The tingle of his balls, the hum in his spine, told him this was going to be mind blowing, but suddenly, Willow stopped and stood up. Jared whimpered.

"Condom?"

It took his fried brain a second or two to sort out what she was asking and when she repeated it, he pointed to the open box on the dresser. She lunged for it and came back to him, ripping one open with her teeth. Jared sat up completely only to be forced back down when she sat across his lap, her legs wide over his.

Shoving her hair out of her face, she tried to roll the condom over his cock. After a second try, he reached up to help her only to have his hands slapped out of the way. When she had him covered, she shimmied up his thighs and rose up over his cock. Jared felt his breath lodge in his lungs.

Her poised over him, juices trailing down her thighs, was perhaps the most erotic thing he'd ever seen. When she didn't move down to take him, he looked up to see her face marred in frustration and tears.

"I don't...I can't...help me, please?"

Reaching for her hands, he laid one on his chest and wrapped the other around the base of his cock. She looked up at him and smiled. Jared's heart flipped in his chest. Then she lowered herself onto him and he forgot how to see.

She gripped his cock in her sheath, the walls tightening, surrounding him, and pulled him deeper. When his cock was seated deep inside of her, she sat up, threw back her head, and began to ride. Jared never took his eyes off of her as she took her pleasure from him.

Her hips moved back and forth, up and down on his body. He watched her, mesmerized by her changes. The way her facial expression told of each discovery of what she was doing, the way her breasts blushed a beautiful pink hue. The sounds she was making, fascinated him. The slap of their skin, slick with sweat, the soft puffs of air, the small moan of pleasure. She chewed on her lip and he remembered them on his cock. Her tongue darted out and he thought about her running it over her nipple.

Her movements became faster now; her breasts jumped and bounced. When her hands moved from over his at her hips up over her tiny waist to her breasts again, Jared sat up.

"Feed me. Give them to me and feed me," he begged.

Her full breasts were lifted as he grabbed her waist. Taking the hard nipple into his mouth, he sucked on only the tip, rolling it onto the roof of his mouth and bringing a moan from deep within her chest. When he paid homage to the other, he felt her tighten around him once again. The more he nibbled, suckled, and laved her, the more frantic her ride became. Running his hand down her back, he cupped her ass to him. Using his other hand, Jared rolled them to her back.

He pounded into her as her climax strangled his cock. Knowing his own was nearly upon him, Jared leaned up over her and hit her deep, each thrust harder than the last. His climax roared through him and he threw back his head and bellowed out her name. Over and over he emptied himself in her. When Willow came again, Jared came with her, his body surging again and again in one of the most powerful climaxes he'd ever experienced.

This time, when he collapsed on her, he knew he was finished. His body was drained and more sated than he'd ever been. He closed his eyes. Rolling to his back and taking her with him, Jared was asleep before he settled on the bed fully.

~Chapter 10~

The pounding at the door woke her. She grabbed the first thing she could touch and pulled it around her. When she realized it was Jared's shirt, she slipped it over her head and opened the door for the food. She had paid by credit card so she only had to pull it from the guy and shut the door. She was on her third slice when she realized Jared hadn't moved.

Pulling out her fourth piece and pouring another glass of pop into the room's only cup, she looked at her one-night stand, Jared Robert.

He knew he could never be anything else to her, or her to him for that matter. Even this, whatever they'd already done, would get her into trouble. But she wouldn't let herself regret what they'd one. She could never do that.

He was beautiful, handsome she supposed men liked to be called. He lay on his stomach now, having rolled to the middle of the bed when she'd gotten up to answer the door. She wondered what he would think of her bed seeing how he slept like he owned the whole thing and she knew that hers would fit him nicely. She immediately stopped that train of thought and moved on to something else. One thing she couldn't do was have him in her home, in her bed.

He went shirtless in the summer, she could see. The dark tan across his shoulders was in deep contrast to the whiter ass cheeks. His long arms, spread wide over the cream-colored sheets of the bed, were furred a light brown. Muscles from hard work and not a workout at a gym flexed in his sleep and she found herself wanting to be held in them.

There was a tattoo over his left shoulder. A dragon in deep reds, blues, and greens was in flight over his scapula and his wings open wide in flight, one over his shoulder, the other nearly touching his spine at mid back. The dragon's tail, long and barbed, wrapped around his bicep and the point of his tail, sharp and lethal-looking, curled down to his elbow.

Willow looked down at her own dragon that flew across the top of her foot, his tail, barbed as well, encircled her ankle and disappeared under her foot.

When Jared stirred, she held her breath, hoping he'd sleep a bit longer. At least until she finished memorizing his body. He settled down again and she was happy to see that the sheet had moved and she could now see his butt and his long legs.

There were dimples at his butt. Deep and wide that seemed to beg to be licked. Mouthwatering at the thought, she drew out the last piece of pizza and bit into it as she tried to imagine what it would be like to wake up next to him every morning, to bite his ass and to taste those dimples. Moving down his body on a heavy sigh, she told herself not to be stupid. She looked at his legs and noticed another tat.

This one was smaller and in script. Standing to get a closer look, she leaned down to see what it said. It was in French and since she spoke that language as well as her own, she had no problem reading what he'd had put there.

"Jamais une femme être doué avec mon amour.

Jamais je donnerai mon cœur à l'autre."

"Never will another woman be gifted with my love. Never will I give my heart to another," she whispered as she sat back down.

Stunned, she knocked her empty pizza box to the floor. She leaned over to pick it up when she heard him roll over again. Looking up, she saw that he was wide awake and he was smiling. Her heart skipped a beat or two before she was able to get herself under control.

"I got hungry and you were sleeping so soundly that I didn't want to wake you. So I ate. My pizza. I ate my pizza. I was hungry." Nerves made her stupid apparently, and she ordered herself to shut up. She looked up when he chuckled.

"You ate an entire pizza? I wondered when you said double the order what you'd meant. You have a healthy appetite."

She glanced down at the opened empty box in her hand and blurted out the first thing that popped in her head. "I worked up an appetite." As soon as the words left her mouth, she felt her face heat up. She dropped her head down and waited for him to laugh at her, but he didn't.

"Come here, Willow, and bring my pizza with you. I want to hold you while I eat." She sat there for several seconds, not moving, but in the end, she grabbed up his box, went to the other side of the bed, and put the box between them.

"It's cold. Maybe we should order you another one." She started to get up, but he grabbed her arm.

"Sit down. This is fine. I don't mind cold pizza. Too bad there isn't any beer. Now that makes a pizza go down smooth."

She watched him sink his teeth into his first slice then watched him chew it. The muscles in his neck worked, tightening and flexing. When a bit of sauce caught in the corner of his mouth and his tongue darted out and licked it away, she groaned. Who knew eating cold pizza could be such a turn-on?

"Willow, if you keep looking at me like that, I'm going to be eating my pizza a great deal colder."

Willow flushed and looked away. "I can't do it anymore tonight. I'm...I'm sore from...from earlier. I know we had a deal, but I don't think...unless you really need to." She chanced a quick look at him and turned away quickly. He was pissed again.

"How sore...look at me please." She turned to see how mad he was. "How sore are you, Willow?"

She bristled. Not at his question, but at the tone. It was soft and inviting. "If you need to do it again, it doesn't matter, does it. Do you? Need it, I mean?" She stood up and pulled his shirt over her head and off. "Just tell me how you want me."

Anger made her voice harsh, humiliation made her body stiff. She was batting a thousand and she just wanted to get out of here. When the half empty pizza box hit the floor, she jumped back and tried to cover her body with her hands. She had a moment to appreciate his semi-hard cock before she backed away from him. He jerked her hands away from her body.

"It's too late for that. Damn it, woman. Do you think I'm an animal?" He shook her. "I asked you a damned question. How sore are you?"

Steeling herself for his fury, she was taken aback by the gentleness of his tone. Then she looked into his eyes. There was fire there, different than before when they had been having sex. Now his eyes were bright instead of dark, but still filled with passion. And even pissed, he was still beautiful.

"Let go of me, Jared. You're hurting me." he released her so quickly that she staggered. When he reached for her again, she backed up. "If you don't require any more sex tonight, then I'd like to go home. I need to be…I have stuff I need to do before work tomorrow."

She felt ridiculous standing there naked in front of an equally naked man discussing work, but she made herself look at his face. Every part of her wanted to taste him again, but she knew that now was not the time. Escape was all she could think about.

"You are the most stubborn woman I…please tell me how badly I hurt you?" She didn't understand why he cared. Most men she knew wanted the woman gone as soon as they were finished. At least that's what she'd overheard the men saying at work.

She turned her head and looked down at the carpet. "I'm sore. I burn when I…when I go to the bathroom, it burns a little."

"Are you bleeding anymore," he asked her softly. That alone made her more embarrassed than telling him that she was sore. Men just didn't ask about those sorts of things. But Willow was beginning to see that Jared wasn't your normal man.

"No. Not since…not since you entered me the first time." She felt the tears threaten to spill. "I'd like to go."

She didn't wait for his answer, but turned and went into the bathroom. She didn't care if he was angry or not, but she needed a minute to herself.

She dressed quickly and gathered her things from the shower. She started to leave the condom on the shower ledge, it was his after all, but was afraid he'd forget it. And since the room was in her name, she didn't want anyone to know what she'd been doing. Stuffing it into her pants pocket, she gathered her things and left the tiny, colorful room.

Jared was dressed and leaning against the dresser when she came out. She wasn't sure what one-night stands did when they parted company, so she stuck her hand out to shake his. He reached out for it and she actually sighed in relief. But it was short lived. He yanked her to him, wrapped his arm around her waist, and held her.

"We aren't finished, Willow. You gave me your virginity and I'd like to know why. Also, I have some questions I want answers to. Who was the man from the other night? Why is it rumored that you and Conley are sleeping together when we both know it's not true?" He pulled her chin up and looked into her face as he continued. "Why did you sleep with me?"

She felt his arms tighten around her when she struggled. She couldn't even look away from his prying eyes because he held her still. She could feel the rigidness of his cock against her belly and stilled when she found herself pressing against him.

"You agreed to no questions." She struggled again. "Let me the fuck go."

The kiss was unexpected, as was the tenderness of it. Willow felt her body betray her by responding. She was achy with need of this man and couldn't understand it. Even her nipples brushing against the inside of her bra felt wonderful. When he lifted his head but didn't release her, she found she didn't mind so much having him hold her, and she wanted to hit something because of it. Closing her eyes, she thought maybe she'd finally gone off the deep end. Then they snapped open when he whispered to her.

"We aren't finished. I still have four hours left of my night. And I—"

"Then get it over with. I'm here now, so fuck me." Please, her mind screamed at him, but she shifted and winced at the slight pull in her muscles. The soreness gave her a quick reminder of why they really couldn't.

"No. Not tonight. We've had entirely too much…fun tonight for you and I'm very sorry about that. But we will. Soon." He let her stand, but he did as well, still not letting her go. "I'll see you tomorrow, Willow. For tonight…well, try and rest up for me."

Lowering his head again, she leaned into him until they were pressed tight against each other. His cock was hard again and she started her hand down the journey of his ribs to touch him. Jared stopped her by pressing his hand over hers. She moaned before she could stop it.

"Not tonight, love. But soon." The whispered promise was made against her lips as she claimed them again.

She was confused. He looked happy that she was leaving, but didn't want her to forget him. He wanted to fuck her, but wouldn't take her because she was sore. Didn't men need to…shifting her bag over her shoulder, she wasn't sure what men needed, but she needed and didn't have a clue how to ask for it. As she stepped through the doorway, his voice stopped her.

"I will get my answers, Willow, and we will finish our night together. I'll see you tomorrow."

She didn't say anything, but stepped out into the chilled night and then drove home.

~o0o~

Jared had to laugh every time Willow practically ran passed the room he was working in. Twice now he'd go in search of her just to see her reaction and it had been well worth it. Even in her anger, she was stunningly beautiful.

He had left the hotel shortly after she had. One, he wanted to make sure she got home safely; two, he wanted to know where she lived. And that had really surprised him

He had her address, of course, but he didn't know the area. He had thought she might live in an apartment or a condo, but she was in a house. And a very beautiful one at that.

Even in the moonlit night, he could tell it was huge. And in what was once a very influential part of town too. The house sat back from the street and had large, well-manicured yards and expensive cars in the driveway.

The curved drive was lined with small trees and flowers, plenty of deep green grass. Jared could tell that work was being done on the house. There was a large dumpster near the garage and it looked like the large structure was being re-roofed.

The house itself was a three story monster with aged brick and shutters. He wanted to come back during the day and have a look at it, but didn't know if she shared the house with someone else or lived with a bunch of hungry dogs. He decided to wait until she invited him over. Then thought he'd be waiting a long time for that to happen and decided he would just show up. He went home a much happier man.

As he waited for the lunch hour to roll around, Jared thought about the woman he'd spent the better part of last night with. The woman was a contradiction. She was sexy and shy, capable and unsure of herself. He'd watched her heft a sixty pound bag of dried plaster over her shoulder to help one of her men and flay the skin off of one of them for doing the same thing. He thought perhaps he could spend hours watching her.

When the signal came to break, he grabbed up his lunch cooler and went to the upper floors to find her. He'd seen her go up about twenty minutes ago and hadn't seen her come back down since. He found her standing near the far window talking on her cell phone. She turned her back on him when he continued into the room and shut the door.

As she continued her conversation, he readied their lunch. Jared pulled two overturned crates over to a large spool of wiring and started pulling out the lunch he'd brought.

"No, that's not what I said, Dad. I said I don't want to come, not that I wouldn't be there. I know what this means to Mom. I'll be there." Jared grinned at her end of the conversation. Seemed their parents had something in common. They wanted their children to remain children.

"Two weeks, three at the most…no, that won't be…Dad, I'm begging you not to set me up anymore. Please? I can find my own dates. No, you didn't say—"

Jared looked at her when he heard she was going to find her own dates. He'd decided last night that he wanted to continue this…well, he wasn't sure what they had going but he wanted more of this woman. A great deal more.

"Look, Dad, I have to go...okay…Yes, I love you too and I know you want only the best for me…Yes, tell Mom I love her as well. Goodbye."

She stood with her back to him, but he knew that she was aware he was still there. When she spoke, she sounded so dejected that he wanted to laugh.

"I don't suppose I could convince you to just go away, could I? I'm having a particularly shitty morning so far and I get the feeling you're going to add to it."

He laughed out loud and realized he had done that a great deal when around her. Laughter was something he'd not done much of when he'd been in Paris.

"No, I'm not leaving. Come here and eat, Willow." She didn't move and he was tempted, too tempted, to get up and bring her back to the makeshift table. Touching Willow James had become addictive and he wasn't sure he thought that was a bad thing.

She turned around and sat down. She picked up the roast beef sandwich that he'd had Beard make for them and took a small bite. Then after that, she plowed into it like a woman who'd not eaten for several days. He watched her push aside the pickle while he polished off his own sandwich, but she did eat the macaroni salad and drank two bottles of cold water. Her appetite amazed him.

Teasing her, he put the last bite of his sandwich on her plate. "You can have that if you give me a kiss."

Her grin made his heart skip several beats. But she only picked it up and popped it into her mouth as her cell phone rang. She didn't pull it out when the sounds of dogs barking chirped from her pocket. He picked up the trash as she sat there and looked at the dirty floor.

"Why have you had a shitty day? You seem to be on schedule here. The last of the drywall is up and the walls are being primed. In another month, you will be on another project and this one will be a memory."

She stood up before she answered. He was glad he was still sitting. "No. No, I won't. This is my last job. I'm quitting after this…if I'm not fired first."

~Chapter 11~

Shawn Talbor watched Will James go into the office, the new guy hot on her ass. He wondered about the guy. Something wasn't quite right about him, but Shawn didn't know what it was. He decided the man wasn't worth his time when he had bigger fish to fry.

His daddy had said that he wasn't going to be bailing him out anymore and that if he fucked up once more then he was going to have to kick him out of the house too. That wasn't going to happen. He had plans for that house once his old man kicked the bucket and getting thrown out wasn't part of his plan. And if he had to take out his dad to stay then what was one more death in the family?

Shawn moved toward the large stacks of piping that was scheduled to go back to the storage area in the morning. He was really glad that he'd overheard Conley tell the bitch that the truck was coming in or he would have been out some grade-a coke. He'd made plans to have the drugs picked up on Saturday, and now the bitch was moving his hiding place out five days early. Leaning over, he was ready to pluck the first of many containers out when Conley spoke behind him.

"That stuff has been counted, Talbor, so if any of it comes up missing, I'll know who to hunt down. You got yourself a little side line going on there where you're selling Stone inventory?"

Shawn had had enough of this nosey bastard and nearly pulled out his gun to take care of him once and for all when he saw Sherman coming toward them. That was another bastard he was taking care of as soon as this was over.

"You're one lucky prick, you know that, Conley? You should buy him a beer. Sherman there just saved you from being dead." Talbor walked away.

He was going to have to come back tonight and when he did, he was going to put the bitch behind a little just to extend his hiding place. He looked up at the big windows in the front of the place. Yeah, that was as good a place as any to start. New windows would have to be ordered and maybe she'd finally get her ass fired over this.

Shawn was walking in his front door to his house when he realized that it was only noon. Not that he did much more than he absolutely need to, but still, he probably shouldn't have left. Shrugging, he made his way to the kitchen. He was hungry again and thought about the pie he'd seen in the fridge two days ago and decided that would make a great snack.

The pie was gone and the only person in the kitchen to take it out on was the little laundry girl. She was cowering in the corner from him when Mason, the family butler, walked in and caught him. Not that the bastard could do anything. He was the master's son after all, but Shawn didn't like to leave witnesses to his work. When Mason pulled him away from the girl on the floor, Shawn started forward again. No one touched him unless he said so.

But Mason was quicker and bigger. Shawn tried to move from the fist that came at him, but he hadn't been eating well and he'd been a little dizzy lately. Yeah, that was it, he'd been dizzy. Staggering to the sink, Shawn reasoned his way to him being the victim and Mason being the bully. He turned to the door when it opened and groaned when his father walked in.

"What's going on here?" Shawn Sr. asked when he came all the way in the room. "Oh my God. Mason, what's he done to her?"

His dad would always believe the worst of him, he realized just then, and Shawn was about to point that out to his father when he slapped him. Twice in ten minutes was more than he could take and he pulled out his gun and pointed it at him.

They all backed up quickly. The stupid cunt on the floor had stopped moving a while ago, but Shawn didn't care. "I didn't do anything. She fell and that's all I want to hear out of her mouth. You, Mason, get over here. You're going to open the door for me and then you're all going to stay right where you are until I'm gone." Shawn started toward the door and looked back at his father. "You try changing the locks on me again and you'll end up in the dirt like my dear old mom."

Shawn drove around for hours before he calmed down enough to try and get a hotel room. He was glad he'd taken the money from his dad's stash. He looked down at the money on his seat next to him and smiled. Stupid bastard probably didn't even know that he knew about it either. His dad was too stupid to live most days and Shawn decided that maybe it was time for him to be retired. Laughing, he pulled up in front of his favorite hotel and went inside. He was still laughing at his own joke when he slipped into the suite and his phone rang.

"It's your dime. Speak to me." Shawn sat down at the little table and pulled out the menu when he realized no one was speaking. "Hello?"

"Where's my merchandise, asshole? You were supposed to deliver yesterday and it is now...two in the afternoon and I still have nothing to sell."

Shawn felt his heart start to pound and his ass start to pucker. He knew that voice and every time he heard it, he hated himself for days afterward. Sweat beaded on his forehead and he could feel it dripping down his back.

"I'm picking them up tonight. There was a problem and I—"

"Do you think I give a shit about your problems, dick weed? No, I do not. You were to bring me my stuff and if I don't have it by midnight tonight, then you will cease to breathe. Do you think I'll have a problem with making that happen, Talbor?"

Shawn closed his eyes. He knew that the man on the other end had no problems in that area at all. Shawn never wanted to be on the receiving end of anything that man had to dish out, ever. Seeing him in action once was one too many times.

"I'll have it. I'll...I'm going to go and get your drugs now—"

The snarl at the other end terrified Shawn. He tried to think what he'd said to piss the man off and realized he'd said the "D" word. No one said drugs over the phone, especially with a cell phone. Shawn didn't say a word. Sometimes less was more, as his mother used to say, and right now, he'd take less of anything.

Shawn pulled the phone from his ear a few minutes later, having not heard anything for a long time, and realized the phone was dead. He hoped that the man at the other end had hung up and Shawn hadn't accidentally hung up on him.

Soaking wet from sweating, Shawn took off his flannel shirt and his pants and walked around the suite in his boxers while he tried to think. He'd never been very good at pressure thinking, but now was not the time for mistakes. He had to get the dru…the merchandise tonight. He was going to have to leave the bitch for some other time and get in and get out before he got another call. Walking to the bathroom, he turned on the cold taps and stepped in after taking off his underwear. It wasn't until he was drying off that he realized he didn't have a change of clothes.

He simply called down at the front desk and had them send him some up from his favorite shop. Shawn then ordered a huge meal and sat down to wait. Pulling out some of the stash from his wallet, he snorted a hit of coke and laid back to wait.

Shawn knew he'd been a bad boy. Even as a kid he'd been into things he shouldn't have. His mother had always found out and every time she had to go to the school or wherever and pick him up, she always tried to make it sound like it was his fault. Well, it hadn't been. Not always anyway. Sometimes he did it on a dare and no one shied away from a dare, not ever.

When he'd been about eight, his mother had slapped him. It hadn't hurt, not really, and she had cried afterwards. But he remembered the humiliation of her hitting him in front of everyone in the kitchen. He vowed that day it would never happen again.

Killing her had been easy. A lot easier than he thought it would be, and he'd gotten away with it. All he'd done was start putting the poison he'd found in the garage into her tea every day. It wasn't his fault that she died; someone shouldn't have left the rat poison out where he could find it. If anyone was to blame, it was the gardener.

He'd thought at the end someone would have noticed that she was getting sicker. He remembered thinking that she was taking too long to die and had doubled the amount he was giving her. Stupid people thought she had died of a lonely heart or a broken one, but he knew. And in the end, she did too. Shawn smiled when he thought about the look on her face when he'd told her what he'd done.

"You shouldn't have slapped me. I don't think you should slap your onlyest child, Mother. That was a bad, bad thing to do."

She was lying in her bed all propped up and staring at him. Shawn smiled at her when she tried to get away from him, even as sick as she was. He lay down next to her as he told her what he'd done.

"So you see, you had to die. But I don't want you to think I didn't learn anything. I did, a lot. I know that killing you was fun, but like Daddy says, all fun must come to an end. But I'll get more practice now that I know how easy it was. And by the time I get old like you, I'll be perfect at it. I will be studied for my methods and when I finally die of old age, they'll find my diary and read how I, a little kid, was able to do the perfect murder." He kissed her on the cheek and laughed when she whimpered. "Goodbye, Mother."

He left the room and went to his own. His mother had lingered for seven more days and in that time, Shawn never once worried about her telling anyone what he'd done. But finally, in the end, he'd given her the straight dose and killed her by putting it under her tongue while she slept.

Shawn looked over at his backpack. In it was another diary and he had several more stashed at his father's house. He'd been keeping notes on the people he killed and really had perfected his craft. His mother had only been the first of many over the years and he had kept track of each and every one of them. Someday, he promised himself; someday, he was going to be famous.

~o0o~

Willow got home just as Jared was pulling up in front of her house. She didn't even want to think about how he figured out where she lived. She just wanted him gone so she could think. Her head hurt from avoiding him all day and now she wanted to take a hot bath, eat some dinner, and go to bed. Her bed. Alone.

He got out of a nice little sports car and then went to the trunk and pulled out three big grocery bags. She didn't care about what he might be doing with those. But when he pulled out an overnight bag, she stormed over to him.

"Good," he said as he shoved a bag in her arms. "You take that one and I can carry the wine. I hope you're hungry."

"I am. But you're not staying. And you certainly don't need a... Hey! Get back here." He simply walked by her as she was speaking to him and she had no choice but to follow.

Marta was coming out and he simply went into the house when she opened the door to leave. He was taking things out of one of the bags when she came inside. He stuffed an olive in her mouth when she opened it to yell at him. Marta laughed as she put her things back on the counter.

She loved stuffed olives and this one was delicious. Chewing fast so that he didn't get too settled before she got him out, he was putting things into her refrigerator with Marta's help when she finally swallowed. Willow began stuffing things back into the bags when he wrapped his arms around her waist and pulled her away from the counter.

"You aren't staying. Just pack up your shit and get out. Or better yet, let me pay you for it and then you can leave quicker. I've had a really—"

The kiss shut her up. She didn't even see him move and suddenly, she was backed against her counter and being kissed senseless by him. As much as she'd told herself she was not going to respond to him again, her body wouldn't listen to reason. He was making her crazy.

When he stopped, it was everything she could do not to beg him to do it again. Something was seriously wrong with her if she couldn't even get one man, a man who worked for her, out of her house. She thought about calling the police, but knowing him, a woman would come and he'd charm her like he was doing to her housekeeper and Willow would end up in jail.

She was still standing there against the counter feeling out of sorts when he handed her a glass of tea. Marta was sitting at the table having a glass of wine and Jared was…what was he doing? Stepping closer to the butcher block, she saw that he was chopping up something green.

"What is that?" Despite her being mad at him and wanting him gone, she was impressed with the way the knife zipped through that thingy with ease. He turned and kissed her on the nose before he answered her.

"This is an artichoke. I'm going to cook us some artichoke and mussel bisque. And by the way, I love this kitchen. Who designed it? I need to find them and have them do a kitchen for me."

"I did it and I'm so not fixing your house for you. I think you should make your soup stuff and go home. I think I have something you can carry it home in somewhere."

She started opening cabinets and then went to the pantry. She knew that here were things to pack crap in; she used them in her lunch when she used to pack it. Coming out of the pantry, she saw that he had moved on to a long green thing and was cutting it up now. Then entire kitchen smelled delicious. And Marta was gone.

She reached around him and took the green thing he was getting ready to chop, or mince, or dice, or whatever the hell he was planning to do with it. He turned to stare at her. "You aren't welcome here. I want you to leave, now, before I call the police." She backed up when he stepped toward her. She didn't like the gleam in his eye. "I mean it, Jared, you should leave here—" The counter stopped her and she watched as he started unbuttoning his shirt.

"I've thought about you all day, you know. I thought about making love with you. I couldn't stop thinking about how you would feel beneath me again." The shirt hit the floor as he stood only a few inches from her.

"You need to...to put your shirt back...Jared..." When his belt came off and ended up on the floor, Willow knew she was in deep trouble.

"Take off your shirt, Willow. I want to taste your skin again." She was shaking her head even as her fingers toyed with the hem of her shirt. "I want to feel your body on mine, under mine."

Both her flannel and the t-shirt she wore under it were suddenly gone. Jared hadn't moved, but her clothing was piled on the top of his. She tried to get him to leave again. He had to be gone soon, before it was too late.

"Jared...Robert, you need to leave my house. I don't allow my employees to come to my home. It's a good...it's a good..." She didn't know how she was supposed to think when he was touching her, and she tried to move away. But somehow, she ended up on the counter with her legs wrapped around him.

"I've thought of you like this. Just like this, Willow." he undid the snap and zipper on her jeans and stepped back to remove them. "Christ, but you are much better in the flesh."

She sat on the counter in her bra and panties. She felt sexy and stupid at the same time. Jared was looking at her with such lust that she couldn't help but feel beautiful. She looked down at what she had on and groaned. Damn it all to hell.

Willow loved sexy under things. When she was feeling particularly down, like she had been this morning, she would pull on her best pair and wear them. No one knew what she had on, well, not normally, but they did give her a nice feeling.

These were a dark blood red. She loved them because they were such a contrast to her skin tone that she felt they made her look like she could be a runway model. When in reality, she was a tall woman who had more muscles than sense.

"You need to leave, Jared. This isn't going to work. We both know—"

The sounds coming from down the hall startled her. The dogs. Marta didn't tell her the dogs were in the house and she didn't have time to open the door now. She hopped off the counter and stood in front of Jared as they came barreling into the kitchen.

"Stay," she said sternly as the door slammed open. But it was too late, they had missed her. And before she knew it, she and Jared were tumbled to the floor and two full grown labs where on top of them.

~Chapter 12~

Jared couldn't believe the dogs. When they had come full tilt into the kitchen, he thought the house was coming down. And when the two of them saw Willow, they had nearly shaken themselves to death to get her to touch them. The three of them were on the back deck now and Jared was finishing up dinner. He looked out the door when he heard her whistle. Smiling, he wondered if he would ever not be surprised by something she could do.

The door opening had him turn. She came in first and then the dogs. She snapped her fingers and they immediately sat down, but were nearly vibrating to get up again. They didn't move as she took off the huge coat that she had grabbed the minute they had untangled themselves from them and ordered them outside. Under the coat, she had on her flannel, the sexy little bra and panty set that he had discovered before they had been interrupted, and a pair of work boots. Jared wanted to peel everything back off her and taste.

"They're beautiful. What're their names?" He looked up from the salad he was making to look at her. "Willow?"

"I didn't name them. I rescued them from a shelter when they were ten weeks old. And the lady there told me that it's bad luck to change a dog's name. She told me it would make them stupid." They both looked over at the dogs who were currently trying to eat each other's tails. "Okay, stupider."

Jared looked at her staring at the dogs. She loved them, he realized. For as much as she called them stupid, she really loved them. But she still hadn't told him their names.

"So what are their names?" he pulled the skillet of curried chicken off the burner and dumped the pasta in a large colander. He looked down at her when she got on the floor with them again.

"The chocolate one is Come Here and the golden one is Damn It."

He nearly bobbled the pot of water when he figured it out. "Their names are Come Here, Damn It? You're making that up." But he could tell that she wasn't.

The dogs, thinking he was calling them, leapt up off the floor and lunged for him. He knew he was a goner and braced for the impact. The shrill whistle brought them to a halt in mid jump. Both of them hit the floor and didn't move. Neither did Jared.

"Bed. Now." And Jared found himself looking for one to climb into. The dogs must have understood they had pissed their mistress off because they left the room with their tails between their legs and heads bowed.

Jared looked at her and fell in love.

The feeling didn't just hit him; it washed over him like a soft rain in a violent storm. He grabbed for the counter and leaned back against it as it came together. Christ almighty, he'd fallen in love. Fallen in love with Willow James. He'd fallen in love so quickly he had no doubt whatsoever that it

104

was real. When he realized she was saying something, he looked at her.

"...today. I don't know why you didn't just go—"

Pulling her to him, he kissed her, claimed her, and conquered her. Her mouth opened under his assault and he took the kiss deeper. When she moved against him, Jared picked her up and sat her back on the counter without breaking contact with her mouth. The buttons on the flannel didn't stand a chance and scattered around the room as he took the barrier off. Sliding his mouth down her throat to her neck, he ran his tongue along her warm skin and laved it. Coming to the strap of her bra, he moved it down her arm as he kissed the skin as he went.

She was delicious, she was hot. Jared wanted her with all his being. Nuzzling her breast through the bit of lace holding her, he bit at the nipple straining hard against the fabric. Her back arched in his hands and he held her still as he moved to the other side, to the other strap, moving it down her, working to free her. When both straps were down on her arms, he took both her hands, put them behind her, and held them.

"Don't touch me. I want to savor you and when you put your hands on me, I lose control." Even he barely recognized his own voice. At her nod, Jared lifted both breasts in his palms, buried his face between the bits of lace, and wrapped her scent around him.

A different kind of need took him. He wanted her, but not just her body. He wanted her. All of her. But even as he suckled at her breast through the cloth, he knew that telling her he loved her would make her panicky, make her bolt. So for now, right this minute, he was going to show her.

Opening the small tab at the front of her bra, he left the cups in place. Taking his time, he watched the heavy orbs fill his hands and he brushed his thumb under the lace just enough to touch her nipples. They were hard and peaked, begging him to take them. He lifted the bra out of his way and stroked them at his leisure. Looking at Willow's face, Jared knew that loving her would make him happier than anything he'd ever done. But he had to follow through on his plan, more so now that he realized he loved her.

"Jared, please. I need you to touch me more. I hurt for you, for your touch."

She didn't move her hands, but the rest of her body canted and rolled against his. Her panties were soaked and though he was still wearing his jeans, he could feel her heat. Moving his right hand down to her belly, he watched the play of emotions move across her face.

His fingers barely skimmed her muscled abdomen, but he could feel them there as they rippled and moved. He brushed his finger against her soft folds and her breath quickened as her legs opened wider. Jared wanted to free his straining cock and drive it into her, but he simply pressed hard on her clit with his thumb once, twice, and then the third time, she came. Before she could fully peak, he pulled away and stepped back.

His body was on fire. His need had tripled when he heard her whimper. His heart pounding hard inside his chest, he took another step back before he trusted himself to speak.

"Dinner is about ready. Will that hold you until we're finished?" he turned his back to her or it wouldn't work.

With a great deal of concentration, Jared started to re-heat the chicken and then serve it onto platters. When he turned back to her, she was still sitting on the counter, her bra hanging at her arms and her panties in place. He had to say her name twice before she focused on him.

"It's time to eat. Are you hungry? If you want to put on another shirt, I'll put things on the table." he moved quickly, not sure what she would do.

The dining room, like the kitchen, was beautiful. The long table in this room had six chairs down each side and one at each end sat on a knotty pine floor. The bright walnut wood gleamed under the huge crystal chandelier that was nearly three feet wide. The walls were cream-colored and the border around the room was simply swirls of deep greens and blues. The built-in glass fronted china cabinet on the left wall was filled with blue and green plates and glasses that matched the set and there were enormous wine and champagne flutes as well. The other cabinet matched in all except the color of the china. In this one, the plates were a holiday pattern, snowmen and trees, Santas and sleds. The glasses were whimsical as well in not only color, but in shape. He had to smile when he saw the small cups and matching saucers that were shaped like snowmen made of marshmallows. Taking out a blue and a green place setting, he was just finishing the table when he heard her come into the room.

She had changed into a pair of sweats and a large sweatshirt. He nearly burst out laughing when he noticed that she had on heavy socks and her hair was pulled back tight from her face. He knew what she was doing and he was delighted that she thought bundling up her body would keep him from it.

"I appreciate you making dinner," she huffed at him. "But when we're done, you have to go. I've got things I have to do tonight and entertaining you isn't on the list." he smiled and went into the kitchen to bring them dinner.

The kitchen was a cook's dream. Not only because it boasted all the most up-to-date appliances, but it was big and open, airy and inviting. The refrigerator was a double wide with a small freezer beneath and an icemaker in the door. The stainless steel front matched the two dishwashers. The counters were a deep sea green tile with a darker green grout. Marta had told him that her mistress had put them in on her own and it had taken her nearly a week to do it. He would bet there were at least thirty feet of counter space along the walls and in the middle isle. The cabinets were glass fronted like the china cabinets in the other room, but these were frosted and well-lit. The stove top, a drop in, had six burners and a deep fryer, he discovered, when he'd removed the covering. He loved working with a gas stove and marveled at how much fun he could have creating.

There was skylight in the ceiling over the island that made the work area filled with natural light. When he'd looked up earlier, he could see that lights, several of them, had been put surrounding the opening, but not so intrusive that they blocked the natural light coming in during the day. The sink and garbage disposal in the counter and woven baskets on shelves beneath made working easier, as did the corner sink in the counters around the walls. Along the wall across from him was a set of built-in ovens, one standard, the other convection.

The other things were vast and unique, as were the decorations that he could see that Willow had added. A large sun dial hung on the wall above the sink; a large cauldron sat on the floor next to the door and held umbrellas. There was a bright painting on the wall that someone had painted there rather than hung and when he looked, it bore the name "James," but nothing more. He picked up the two platters of food and backed his way into the dining room. He was about to start phase two of what he had called "Willowgate."

~o0o~

Like everything else she did, Willow ate with gusto. She had planned to eat quickly and make him leave, but the meal was so delicious that she found herself lingering over it just to savor it. He drank a glass of wine while she had tea, and her salad had dark olives while his did not. How he had figured out she loved olives was beyond her, but she liked that he had gone to the trouble. When the dinner was over, she went to get the pups.

"How long have you had them? They are very well behaved when they realize you're staying, aren't they?" She looked up at him from petting Here and he was giving the same lavish treatment to It.

"About six months. They had been dropped off at the shelter with name tags on them and a note saying they were just too much. I contacted the previous owners before I took them and she said that she didn't realize that puppies could be so much work and she lived in an apartment. And after her sleaze boyfriend had named them and dumped them on her, she couldn't really afford to keep their care up anymore either." She sat back in her chair and watched Jared do the same. "They were in good health and they aren't that much trouble."

"Marta helps you, I suppose, with them, I mean. It's a beautiful house, Willow. How long have you owned it?"

She looked around. Yeah, it was becoming a beautiful house. "Ten years. I bought it from the city when they were renovating this area. Several of the houses had been slated for demolition, but this one and three others came up to code but needed a…they said work, but it was more like a rebuild. But I've had fun. And in a few years, I'll sell it and move to the next project."

"I'll buy it. I don't care what you're asking, I'll buy it. Hell, I'll buy it now. It's perfect for what I want."

She laughed. "You've only seen this floor, Robert. For all you know, the rest of the house could be shit. I've got four of the bedrooms finished, but there are several more. Plumbing is complete, as is the wiring, but the walls aren't. I work on it when I can now, and more later. The roof I hired out to finish. It was too high for me and I know very little about shakes roofs.

He stood up and held out his hand. "Show it to me."

Did she want him in her house? No. Not really. Okay, she did. It was tempting to just tell him it was time to leave, but if he wanted to see it then she would show it to him, the things that only another person who worked construction might see. She didn't want to admit it, but she wanted his opinion too.

"All right, but then you leave. I mean it. I have to get things ready and you're a major distraction." His laugh made her realize how that sounded, but she left it alone.

They carried their dinnerware into the kitchen and put everything on the counter. He let the dogs out to play while she filled their dishes. When they all came back in, he had a dusting of snow on him.

"It's snowing? It's only October." She ran to the door and looked out. It hadn't stuck yet, but it was coming down in big, fluffy flakes. Willow loved the winter more than any other season. Pulling herself away, she led him out of the kitchen from the door opposite of the dining room.

"This is what my mom calls the family room. I call it my room. The walls aren't finished yet, but I think in a few more weeks I'll have them primed and ready. The wallpaper in here was hideous."

The room was large and full of second hand furniture that her parents had given her. The big screen television hung over the mantle, but had not been on all that much. She usually had things to do when she got home and if she made it as far as this room before going up to bed, she just read a book or something. The dogs had claimed the area in front of the gas fireplace when she'd first brought them here and that's where they went now. Jared sat on the couch and patted the seat next to him.

All sorts of alarms went off in her head. If she sat next to him, he'd touch her. If he touched her again like he had in the kitchen, she would be begging him to stay. Walking around the couch, she sat in the double wide recliner and sat back. She didn't like it when he laughed.

"Afraid, Willow? You don't strike me a woman who would be afraid of a man."

"I'm not afraid of you. I just like this chair. It's comfy. I thought you wanted to see the house."

She had actually never sat in this chair, but she wasn't going to tell him that. When he stood, she swallowed hard. She could see his cock outlined against his jeans and he looked very hard.

When he stood next to the chair, she found herself sitting up straighter. If she were to tilt her head just a little, she could take him into her mouth and taste him again. Yesterday just had not been enough. Clearing her throat, she looked over to the dogs, who were sleeping.

"Willow, stand up please." Her heart began pounding and she could feel her body ready for him. She didn't look, but knew he was holding out his hand.

"You should go, Robert. I don't think this—"

"I would very much like it if you called me Jared when we're not at work. I like hearing my name pass over your lips. Especially when you shout it while you climax. Please come here."

Standing up, she was only a few inches from him. But she could feel his warmth, smell his cologne. He smelled like the outdoors and male. Willow wanted to bury her nose in his neck and take his scent into her body. Steal it way and be able to pull it out when she needed to and think about his touch, his kisses, his taste.

He pulled her into his arms and she went willingly. She pressed to him as he aligned their bodies and moaned when his lips brushed over hers before kissing her deeply. She loved the way he could kiss her and make her lose all reason. Even the barest of touches could make her sway with need. When he put his hands on her ribs, she reached up and wrapped hers around his shoulders then around his neck. Even as the kiss deepened more, he didn't move his hands, didn't touch her more. Just when she thought she'd expire from need, a buzzing sounded. Jared pulled away from her and then took a step back. Willow dropped her hands when he dropped his.

He pulled out his cell phone and pressed a few buttons then put it away. "I have to go. My time is up."

"Now? You have to go right now?" her body was screaming at her. Her mind was mired in lust. He couldn't leave her like this.

"Yes. My time is up. I only had four hours and that's over." He turned away from her and went to the door while she simply stood there. "I'm sorry about the kitchen. I'd help you clean it up, but…" He disappeared into the kitchen and a few minutes later, she heard the door to the outside open then close. When his car started, she sat down hard on the chair. He left.

He had left her.

~Chapter 13~

Jared pulled over when he was about a mile from her house. He put the engine in park, leaned back against the head rest, and took several deep breaths. It didn't help. He could smell her on his clothes, on his skin, and she was making him hurt, ache without her even being here. Leaning his head on the steering wheel, he had to chuckle. It was that or cry.

He was beginning to see the flaw in his plan. In getting her worked up to the point where she begged him to stay, he was also worked up. He was wound so tight right now that if she were to brush her finger over his cock, he'd come. Looking down at himself, he wondered how long a man could go without exploding from not coming. He hoped that he wouldn't have to find out. He was hurting enough now.

Putting his car back into gear, he thought about the evening. She had wanted him, and had he stayed for one minute longer, he was sure he would have begged her if he could. But he wanted her to make the decision. She needed to ask him to stay. He'd hoped that he could get her to the bedroom before he'd left her, but the room where he'd kissed her was so her.

He felt badly about the mess he'd left her and he didn't doubt she'd clean it up before going to do whatever it was she kept telling him about. He opened the window on his car to let the cold rush over him. When he got home he was going to need a cold shower quick. Maybe several of them.

~o0o~

Willow put the last glass in the dishwasher and closed it up. Looking around the kitchen, she could see that everything was just the way it had been. Hanging up the towel on the rack, she went to the dining room again and turned off the lights. It was the first time the room had been used since she finished it and the furniture had been delivered two weeks ago.

Moving with the dogs on her heels, she took them to the mud room and told them to go to bed. They were good dogs and she loved them dearly and they obeyed her at once. She thought about Jared's reaction to their names and smiled. It was pretty much the same one she'd had. Closing their door to their room/laundry room, she made her way to the front of the house and set the alarm. Going up the stairs, she went first to the spare bedroom to check to see if she had what was needed. Satisfied, she closed and locked the door behind her and went to her office.

It was nearly an hour later when her phone rang, startling her out of a daydream of Jared and not working. She snatched it up, hoping it was Jared, but knew it was impossible because he didn't have the number. But she smiled at her mom's greeting.

"I'm going to murder your father. I have never been so— shush up. I'm talking to my daughter."

Willow knew that in a few seconds her father would pick up the extension in their home and tell her his side of the story about whatever had made her mom mad. It was a little longer than she thought before he did it.

"I can't believe you hid the phones, Mandy. That was just childish. Hello, darling daughter, how's my favorite little girl?"

Willow grinned. That explained the delay somewhat. But she still didn't know what had prompted the call at midnight.

"I'm your only daughter, Dad, and I'm fine. What did you do to Mom to tick her off?"

He snorted. "Why do you assume that I made her mad? Maybe she made me mad. Did you think of that?"

"If Mom would have done something to make you mad, you would have called first, not her. She's the injured party this time, not you. What did you do?"

"It was an innocent mistake. All I did was—"

"Innocent," her mother shouted at them both. "Do you know how long I had that magazine? I was keeping that article for later and you threw it away."

"Darling, the date on the front said March of—" her dad started only to be cut off by her mom.

"Don't you dare darling me you pompous ass. I know darn good and well what the date was on it. I purchased it, didn't I?"

Willow burst into tears. She hadn't meant to, but it was just too much. The magazine incident was forgotten and both parents were totally focused on her. She didn't want that, but she was glad they had stopped arguing. Willow started babbling before she could get control of herself.

"He just left me. Not even another kiss. And the dogs liked him. How could they betray me...why would he not make love to me again? I was right there. I know I was a bit overdressed, but he didn't have any trouble taking them off. Am I ugly?"

She started crying again and held the phone tightly to her ear. Her mom was comforting her and her dad was not saying much, but she knew he was there. It was a full five minutes before she could speak again without bursting out again. Her dad said he was going to hang up and let her talk to her mother.

"Are you all right, darling? Why don't you come home? Bring those two idiots with you and they can run in the fields. I won't even care if the track mud in the house again."

Willow laughed. She was sure that's what her mom had wanted. The dogs were terrified of her mom and with good reason. She had smacked them both good on the butt about a month or so ago for coming into the house with muddy feet. Willow didn't know how her mom expected them to wipe their feet, but she would bet her last buck the dogs would try before they disappointed her again.

"I'm sorry. You probably got more than you bargained for in that. I'm going to be fine. I'm just tired. You know how it gets this close to the end of a project."

Amanda James was an architect. M. James to those who she worked with and Mandy to her friends. She had inspired Willow to do what she did. Mandy's buildings were world renowned and she had designed the last ten hotels her family had built. Not to mention several others that kings and queens lived in as well as two former presidents.

"Yes. I heard that you told your dad you'd be finished in a little over two weeks. Are you still on schedule to finish early?" Willow smiled. Her mom was waiting on her to speak first of the mystery man. "I bet you're proud of your crew. That will set well for your future jobs."

"Yes. The man who we're building it for is a bit odd, but he knows what he wants. We did have a problem with the floors in the employee dining room, but he let me keep it that way."

Mandy snorted. "You mean you convinced him to see it your way. Good girl. So, tell me about your next project. Are you staying with Stone Construction?"

Willow closed her eyes. "He didn't hurt me, Mom, he just left me. I was hurt because I thought…well, it doesn't matter what I thought. It's over. Yes, it's over, and I'm happy it is."

"What sort of relationship were you having with him besides sexual? I mean, you said he was at your house. There has to be more than just sex for you to have him to your house."

Frowning, she shifted in her chair. "Why do you say that? I mean, I know I keep it private, but that doesn't mean I'm not unknown. Some of the men know where I live."

"Sweetheart, just because one or two of them follow you home when you work late does not mean they know where you live. You haven't had a single person there since you bought it other than construction workers and those few and far between. I doubt you've had the cable people out and the monstrosity of a television is still not hooked up."

Willow thought of the television in her family room and frowned. No, it wasn't hooked up, but she'd been busy. Of course Marta could have waited for them, but that wasn't the point.

"We aren't really having a relationship so much as he wanted to fulfill a bargain we had stuck up and I wanted more. As for him coming here, I didn't invite him, he just showed up with all this food. And he cooked it. No one has ever cooked for me…why am I telling you this? It's over. He's happy and I'm happy. End of story."

Her mom was quiet for some time before she spoke. "Wills, this has nothing to do with the comment your brother made the other week, does it? I don't think he meant for you to go out and find someone to sleep with."

Willow was hurt by the comment, but then realized that her mother had only asked because she loved her, not because she thought Willow would do it. But had she? She didn't think so. Not the way the two of them had come together.

"No. He's just...he works for me. It's probably just as well that it's not going anywhere. If we got caught, and you know I will, then it could mean both our jobs. I think him leaving was for the best."

Then why did it hurt so much? After a few more minutes of going over plans she was working on for her house, Willow hung up. She went down the hall to her bedroom, stripped down to her panties, and climbed into bed. Her last thought before she drifted off was that she was glad he'd not gotten in her bed. She didn't think she'd ever be able to get his scent out of it.

~o0o~

Mandy looked up when her husband of thirty-five years walked into the library. She was still a little mad at him, but their daughter was more important right now. She smiled when he took her hand into his and kissed the back of it.

"Did that article mean that much to you or was it the signature on it that had you so upset?"

Mandy looked at him. "You know it was. She signed it for me the day the stupid thing came out. And even though she had been upset because the interviewer had made her sound like a silly girly girl, she read every word to me. Which she was not, she said. Why do you ask? Are you trying to make me pissed again?"

He stood up, picked up the cushion he'd been sitting on, and pulled out the very magazine they'd been fighting about. She took it from him and held it to her chest. With tears in her eyes, she looked at him. "Willow signed her name on this the day I brought it home. She said she had never signed her name with meaning before." She lifted it from her and looked at the cover with her daughter's face looking back at her. "She was thirteen and just graduated from high school and in her first year of college when they took this. She'd wanted to have her hair dyed and I wouldn't let her. She wanted to look older."

"She said that you told her someday she'd look at this cover and wonder where the little girl had gone." Edgar took her hand again and kissed it. "I hid it so we could fight and then have make-up sex."

Mandy burst out laughing and realized that her daughter sounded just like her. Mandy leaned over and kissed him on the mouth quickly. Then looked at the photo again.

"She's in love, Edgar. I don't think she knows it, but she is. She would never have given herself to someone if she wasn't. She has too much respect for herself not to."

Edgar leaned his head on her shoulder and sighed. "So, when are we leaving for Ohio? Tomorrow, or do you think we should wait for the weekend?"

Mandy smiled. He knew her so well. "Friday is good. I have that meeting with the board of directors at the shop at two. We can leave right after."

~*Chapter 14*~

Shawn parked two blocks over from the site and got out his flashlight. He had to get in and get out before the fucking truck came to get the stuff or he was going to have to drive to the storage place and get it from there. If he had to do that, he was not going to be happy.

He'd fallen asleep just and had forgotten to set his alarm. He'd wanted to get the merchandise out before dark so that he could get this over with. Now here he was at five in the fucking morning, walking along a dark street doing it.

There were no lights on at the office for which he found himself both happy about it and pissed. That meant that the bitch wasn't working and he could make as much noise as he wanted, but where the hell did she get off not being to work early? He wanted to cause some serious damage to that bitch and would before it was all over. He moved to the back of the lot to where the extra shit was stored. He was there for twenty minutes before he realized it was gone. Everything had been moved. Shawn even went to the front of the lot where they stored the big equipment and none of it was there either.

Shining his light around again, he realized that she had had it picked up just to fuck him over. Shawn walked to the office and pounded on the door. He wasn't sure why, but he wanted the bitch right here to explain to him why she couldn't follow a fucking schedule when she set it up. She was going to pay. As soon as he found her, he was going to make her pay. Heading to his car, his phone started ringing and without even looking, he knew who it was.

"Do you have any fucking clue as to what time it is? Or do you even want to continue as you have in this world?" The voice cracked with anger.

"I'm going to pick it up now. I had a...I'm coming, just wait." Shawn took off at a run to his car. He was completely out of breath when he got there and had to lean on the car for a few minutes to calm his pounding heart. "I'm driving to where it is right now."

"No you're not, fuck-tard. You're leaning against your car trying not to have a fucking heart attack. Do you honestly think I'd not have you tailed?" The laughter moved over his body and produced sweat. "Get in that piece of shit you drive and go. I don't have all fucking night."

Shawn looked around as he opened his door. Terror was his new best friend and he didn't even know his name. It took him three tries to get the keys in the ignition then another two times to get the key to turn. He kept the phone to his ear because frankly, he was afraid not to. He knew where the storage lot was, but got lost twice because he missed the street trying to figure out if the cars behind him were following him or not. By the time he pulled in the parking lot, he was soaking wet with sweat and he had the shakes bad. Pulling out his own stash...well, a little of the stash he was supposed to be delivering for the man on the phone, he took a heavy snort.

Instantly, he felt the rush. Throwing back his head, Shawn sat there waiting for his body to catch up to the rest of him. Suddenly feeling like he could conquer the world, he got out of his car and sauntered up to the fence surrounding the storage for JR Stone Construction. He turned around just before he touched the fence when blue and red lights reflected off the building next to him.

"Wouldn't do that, buddy. That fence is wired and it'll knock you clean into next week if you touch it."

Shawn looked back at the fence and noticed the "high voltage" and "danger" signs posted in front of it. Taking a hasty step back, he looked to see if The Voice was close enough to hear this and was sure he'd known about the fence too. Everybody was out to get him. Sliding his gun out of the back of his pants, Shawn leaned down to look at the cop and was startled to see one in the passenger seat and two more in the back seat.

What the fuck? Was there a shortage of patrol cars so they all had to come in one car? Carefully, he slid the gun behind him and up under his coat. He might be high, but he knew that he'd be able to shoot one of the cops, maybe even two. But there was no fucking way he could kill all four of them.

"Thanks, officer. I was here to check out something for the boss lady. Seems she's too lazy to get her ass outta the bed and come check it out by herself. She didn't tell me there was electricity running through it. Maybe she wants me into next week." Shawn laughed, as did the cops. "Yeah, good thing you came around when you did."

"We had a report of somebody walking around the back side of the fence. So to keep the peace, we decided to put some extra patrols out over the next few days."

Fuck! Now he'd have to come back and watch for cops. That stupid bitch was going to pay and she was going to pay sooner rather than later. Nodding his good night to the cops, he moved back to his car the indirect way.

Shawn knew he was fucked if he couldn't get the merchandise. He had fifty pounds of pure uncut coke stashed for The Voice and knew the man was not going to be waiting around forever. Three point five million was a lot of merchandise.

He didn't answer his phone. He didn't want to hear that he was going to die again. He'd have to make up some excuse to get to the storage yard tomorrow. Well, he supposed today now. Going back to the hotel seemed to him to be a really stupid move so he drove around until he found an out of the way cheap place and stayed there. It was the ugliest place he'd ever seen, but he felt safe.

~o0o~

Tuesday morning Willow was in the trailer at nine in the morning when Jared went to find her. He was ready to launch phase two of Willowgate and she'd been hiding in the office long enough. He pounded on the door and waited for her to come and unlock the door. When she shouted to come in, he was pissed again. Damned woman.

"I thought I told you to lock the door when you were in here. Do you want just anyone to barge in here?"

"Somebody already did. Don't you have something to do? I'm kind of busy here." her tone was clipped and he might have smiled if he wasn't afraid she'd see him. "It was my understanding that the last of the walls needed to be primed before the painters could show up."

Nor was she looking at him. Jared sat in the chair and looked at her. Her hands were a little shaky and she was fumbling with the papers on her desk. Finally, she looked at him and glared.

"You look very lovely this morning. Can I kiss you?" Jared stood to do just that when she licked her lips. "And I was wondering if I could come over and cook for you again? You can't believe how much fun I had."

She didn't move away from him when he turned her chair. Leaning down, he braced his hands on the arm rests on either side of her chair. Her breath was warm and he wanted to toss her over the desk and take her, but knew that he had to do this slowly. With a quick kiss on her mouth, he stood up and moved back to the other chair. She looked so confused he wanted to laugh.

"Willow, you didn't answer my question. Can I?" She was slow to respond, but he was learning he was a patient man. Leaning back in the chair, he knew that she would be his before this week was out. If not...well, Jared might not live past the week really. He'd never ached so much for a woman in his life.

"Why?" he waited for her to say more.

"Why what? You mean the kitchen? Well, it's a cook's dream and I love to cook. I have the biggest collection—"

"No. Why are you doing this to me? I don't understand you. You come in my house, make me crazy with need, then walk out as if we'd done nothing more than eat that curry stuff you cooked."

"Didn't you like the curried chicken? I could make anything you'd like, you know. I thought about making us Philly cheese steak san—"

Her growl stopped him. Biting the inside of his cheek, he was sure he'd have a permanent place there to keep from laughing at her. It really wasn't funny, he supposed, but he couldn't help himself.

"Did you find me lacking? I know that I didn't know what I was doing, but I could learn, you know." She turned away from him before she continued. "I guess that I should have taken lovers when I was in college, but it just didn't seem right. Plus, I was...you know, it doesn't matter. I'd rather you didn't come over any more. But thanks all the same."

The door opened before he had a chance to answer her. It was Talbor. Jared could very easily knock the man on his ass, but held back. He should have fired the bastard when he'd first come on site, but then he wouldn't have gotten to meet Willow.

"Well ain't this just cozy? The boss lady and the new guy all closed up in the office together. Whatever will the owner think? Maybe I should just call him up and let him know you're fucking someone on company time."

Before Jared could react, Willow stood up and came toward the man. He was bigger than Willow, but Jared would bet any amount of money she could be meaner. But she could still get hurt because Jared knew that Talbor wouldn't fight fair.

"If you have something to say, then say it. I'm done with you coming in here making noise about calling the owner. Do it, I don't give a flying fuck." She picked up the bat next to the door and pointed it at him. "Either tell me what you want or get the fuck out of here."

Red-faced, Talbor stood his ground. Jared was suddenly afraid for her. He could see the slight insanity in Talbor's eyes and thought the man was high. But when he started to stand up and throw him out, Willow brought the bat down on his shoulder and let it lay there.

"You fucking bitch, one of these days I'm going to find you without that bat then what are you going to do?" Talbor turned to Jared next. "And you, you suck-wad, you're going to be next. This company is going to be mine and you won't have a cozy little job any more. I came in here to ask you about the storage shit. Where the fuck is it? I was sent to get some of those pipes to replace the one that got bumped and they're gone."

"Bumped? How the hell did one get bumped? Whatever. Everything is at the storage yard." She pulled out her radio, but put it back. "Tell Conley to go over and get it. He has a key. You get that plaster work done on the main hallway?"

"No. Can't be everywhere at once. I'll tell Conley, but I ain't your fucking messenger boy. Next time, you do it." he left without another word.

Jared didn't move when she went back to the desk. This time, she was leaning against it and not moving. He stood up, walked up to her, and pulled her up from the desk. Then he took her into his arms, kissing the top of the head, and he lifted her chin up.

"I'm coming over tonight and we're going to have a great dinner. Then when we have the kitchen cleaned up, I'm going to make love with you. Then when we're finished, I'm going to make love with you again and again."

She looked up at him and smiled and Jared's heart flipped over. "Jared, I'm not sure this is such a good—"

He'd meant for the kiss to be tender. He'd meant to just brush his lips over hers and then go back to work, but he'd denied himself for too long. He'd denied them both for too long. Before he knew it, he had her pressed against the filing cabinet and his hands filled with her ass. His phone ringing brought them both crashing back to earth.

"I have to take this. Fuck, I want you." he kissed her again and walked to the door. "I don't think I can wait for dinner then clean up. I'm going to take you on the floor as soon as I get there then we can eat. Maybe."

Jared stepped out of the office and into the bright sunlight as he answered the call. This was going to be the longest day of his life.

"Hello, Dad, what's going on?"

~Chapter 15~

Daniel Smyth, not his real name, nor was The Voice as Talbor called him, closed the file he'd been looking at and regarded the man across from him. His lawyer, Jack Spencer, had gone to a great deal of expense to get him this information and it had been well worth it. Daniel knew that Talbor called him The Voice and thought it was funny.

"How much of my merchandise has he stolen that you know of? And is there any way to get it back?"

Jack pulled out another folder and flipped through it. "He's managed to get about half of it, but the rest is still in the lot. I'm not sure how much longer you should let this idiot work for us. He's going to get us in trouble."

Daniel didn't plan on Talbor working for them much longer, but he was going to get his dope back from him if it was…well, it was going to be the last thing he did. His death was going to be tragic.

"Keep an eye on him." Daniel looked down at the file again. "The woman he keeps blaming for his screw-ups, is she as involved as he said she is?" He pulled the picture of her taking drywall off a flatbed truck. She didn't strike Daniel as anyone who would involve herself with trash like Talbor, but the world was a crazy place.

"Willow James. No, she's not involved with him. She and this guy here,"—a picture came across his desk—"Jared Robert, are semi involved. He's been to her house a couple of times. Not sure what his connection to Talbor is, but from all accounts, he hates the man as much as she does."

Daniel glanced at the second man's face. If he wasn't involved then he didn't care. He had enough going on right now to be worrying about some guy trying to bop his boss.

"Where is Talbor now, do we know?" Jack nodded. "Good. Keep a tail on him and make sure that he doesn't leave town. I'm going to pay him a little visit tomorrow night. I want Carter to come with me. Make sure he knows that I want damage, but nothing permanent. I want this prick to be able to walk but not run."

"And the woman? What should we do about her? She did have the merchandise moved without telling him." Jack didn't like women and Daniel knew this.

"If you're sure she's not involved, it could have been as simple as moving it when she had the chance. If she is involved…well, I will take care of her personally."

After Jack left, Daniel picked up the file again and stared at the faces of the three people he'd had planted there. Two of them were worthless, Talbor being one, and one other was beginning to be a little itchy for his tastes. Louis was starting to act like he wanted out and Daniel couldn't have that. When a person signed on for him, then he or she signed on for the duration.

The third guy was gone. Daniel was sure that Talbor had something to do with the disappearance of Bailey, but had no proof. But Talbor had said things, hinted at things that made Daniel sure of it. Plus, he thought the man was slightly, if not over the top, insane. Daniel was going to enjoy taking the man out.

Getting up from the desk, he went to the wall of books, pulled the copy of "*The Raven*," and waited until the entire wall moved from its resting place. He slipped behind it before it was completely opened and then started the process to have it go back into place. Smiling, he made his way down the stairs to the lower levels.

"Hello, sir," Daniel said to the room just beyond him "We have and issue with Talbor."

"Fuck," was the reply. "What's the fucking idiot done now?"

"The merchandise had been moved to a storage area and now has cops surrounding it. He's not about to get to it." Daniel moved to one of the easy chairs. "He needs to be gone."

"I agree, but let him hang himself. Give him until he gets the merchandise. Maybe a cop will save us the cost of a bullet and kill him for us."

Daniel nodded and thought things were beginning to look up.

~o0o~

Willow was nervous. Not just nervous, but actually terrified. Jared would be here any minute and she didn't know what to do with herself.

"You had better sit down, Wills, or you'll be worn to a frazzle before he gets you to bed."

Willow stared open mouthed at Marta. "How did you...what are you talking about? He's coming over to cook dinner, that's all."

Marta mumbled something under her breath then looked up from the laundry she was folding. "He looks at you like you're an all-day sucker and he can't wait to lick him a few bites of you."

Willow blushed. She didn't know what to say because she knew that's what he wanted to do to her too. She sat down in the kitchen chair and started sorting socks. Marta brought her laundry over to do when she did Willow's. She didn't care that Marta used her washer and dryer. It meant that she didn't have to do it.

"How do you know this stuff? I mean, he is coming over, but as far as the sex goes…" Willow took a deep breath before asking the older woman. "I'm not very good at it. Maybe he's coming over to just…you know…get off. You think?"

Marta cackled. Willow started to get up and leave, thinking she'd call him up and tell him not to come over. She was to the phone when Marta wrapped her arm around her waist and pulled her into her embrace.

"Honey, he don't care how good you be at sex. Besides, he seems like a man who knows how to treat a woman in bed, so whatever he wants you to know, I'm sure he would be the one to teach it to you."

Willow watched Jared pull up next to her garage and begin to unload bags from his trunk. Then he pulled out a duffle bag.

"He wants to spend the night with me. What if he—"

Marta cut her off. "And if he do then you try and do it to him. He's a good man, that one. You just be yourself and I think you will be good."

Marta was pulling on her coat when Jared came in the kitchen door, the dogs right behind him. Willow took the dogs to the family room after telling Marta goodbye. Willow sat on the couch with Here and It for a few minutes. She saw Jared leaning in the doorjamb when she looked up.

"Come here, Willow. Please?"

She looked down at the fire she'd turned on in the fireplace instead of looking at him. "I had Marta make us some things that would keep. They're in my bed...my room. I have a refrigerator in there. There're also some things to drink."

She stood up and so did he. She wasn't sure what to do now, but commanded the dogs to follow her. Jared moved to the side when they passed him. She pulled down the dog food and was about to open it when he took it from her.

"Get their water and I'll do this. Will they be all right until morning? Or will they need to be let out again?"

She picked up their dishes and walked into the kitchen. "No, I'll come down and let them out later. It's something we do. There's a treat on the shelf above your head. Give them each one if they go to their bed without you telling them."

Willow only put them in this room when they were to go to bed. They had never quite gotten it, but she tried. When first Here then It ran to their beds for Jared, she wanted to both smack them and praise them. Jared gave them their treats and shut the door behind him.

Now she was nervous again. Picking up the bags that he'd brought with him, she began folding them. Then she picked up the washcloth on the sink and began scrubbing the counter tops. When he came up behind her, slipped his arms around her, and took the cloth, she found herself leaning back against him.

"I'm not going to hurt you, Willow. And we certainly won't do anything you don't want to." He kissed her neck and nothing more. "Tell me what you want, love. Tell me."

She turned in his arms and wrapped hers around his neck. "You, I want you."

Willow knew that what they had wasn't going to last. She didn't have any doubts that a man like him would become bored with someone as inexperienced as her and soon. But she knew something he didn't. She had fallen in love with him sometime in the last hour. It was when he'd helped her take care of her dogs that sealed the deal. Taking his hand, she went to the alarm system and gave him the number so that he could leave if he wanted. He grabbed up his duffle before they left the kitchen.

"Just set the number and hit 'exit.' It will reset it so that everything is buttoned down when you leave. The rest of the house is already locked up."

Before she could move from the door, he turned her and pressed her back against it. The kiss was soft and gentle and took her breath away. Before she could pull him closer and kiss him back, he stepped back and took her hand.

"I'm not leaving tonight. Tomorrow morning I want to make love to you again before we go to work then after we're finished for the day, I'll come back here and fix dinner then make love to you again."

She nodded. The thought of him being next to her all night was making her giddy. Turning, she led him upstairs to her room. She opened the door and let him go in first.

"Christ. I'm going to have a lot of fun in this bed with you. Where did you get this thing?" he sat on the edge and bounced twice. "Oh yeah, this is going to be fun. Come here."

"I had it made. I noticed when we...from the other time we...You take up a lot of bed when you sleep. I thought about you here." She turned away when she realized what she'd said. "I'm sorry. I'm not very good at this."

Jared stepped in front of her and lifted her chin. "It's very cute how you get shy on me. You know what I think about when I think of that night in the hotel? You riding me. Your head thrown back in ecstasy while you took me deep inside of you. The way your breasts swayed and moved as you did. The way you felt wrapped around me."

Her breath shuddered and she couldn't think. At least not about anything but the things he was describing. She'd thought about her taking him too, but she hadn't thought about how he had enjoyed it. Now it was all she could think about.

"Come to bed with me, Willow. Come and let me love you."

He led her to the bed. Cupping his hands at her face, he kissed her gently. She had no idea that there were so many different kinds of kisses that a couple could share. She only knew that he was an expert at all of them. When his hands slid down her back, cupped her ass, and brought her to him, she felt the hard evidence of his need.

He pulled his mouth from hers, stepped back, and looked at her. "Undress for me. I want to watch you."

Jared sat on the edge of her bed again and Willow tried to figure out how to take her clothes off without looking stupid. Then she realized it didn't matter how she felt. It was him she wanted to please.

"I have this fetish for under things. Silk is my favorite, but I like leather too." When she had all the buttons undone on her shirt, she dropped it on the floor behind her. Talking helped her be less nervous about messing up. "I don't have any dresses. Well, I have one black one, but that's just for emergency. I have some black thigh-highs that I wear with it."

She left on her t-shirt and started on the buttons of her pants. These were the dressiest pants she owned and the holes where the buttons slipped into were tight. It took her a moment or two to get them through. The popping open of each button seemed loud in the room.

"I'd like to see you in thigh-highs. And a garter. I want to take you sometime when you have on just those stockings and a garter." Jared's voice sounded strangled and while she watched, he lay back on the bed and opened his own pants. "Don't stop."

The image of him taking her over the end of the bed with just her garter and stockings on made her wet. She looked at the end of the bed and could almost see them there. Him behind her, naked and slamming deep into her. She looked back at him when he groaned.

"That's where I want you too. Christ, I want you. Please, Willow, take off the rest so I can see if you have on leather or silk. You're killing me."

Empowered by his apparent need, she started to shimmy out of her pants. He wanted her and that alone made her feel wonderful. When she was down to her panties, bra, and t-shirt, he shimmied his jeans down to his hips. His cock was stiff and thick and her mouth watered to take him in. Licking her lips, she started to take off her panties when he stopped her.

"No. The shirt. Take off your shirt first. Let me see you." She pulled it over her head and tossed it on the floor with her other things.

The leather had been cool against her skin when she'd put it on tonight. Now it felt tight and hot. The softness of it rubbed against her hard nipples and she reached up and cupped her breasts to rub them more. His harsh groan had her stop.

"Don't stop. Pull it…pull it down so that your nipples are exposed. I want to watch you lick them again." She did as he asked. "Christ, Willow, come here."

He sat up and pulled her forward by grabbing her hips. The tiny strings there came loose in his hands and he pulled them away from her body. When his hand came up between her thighs, she trembled with need and she wondered how long she could stand. His fingers entered her as he took her into his mouth.

Her climax was fast. Knowing that no one could hear her, she screamed out his name. She did it with wild abandonment. Wrapping her fingers into his hair as he ate at her, she held him to her. The waves of pleasure rolled over her; tiny explosions detonated all over her body, her breasts, nipples, even her knees felt them. Just when she wasn't sure she could stand any longer, he lay back down and started to pull his pants off the rest of the way.

"Hurry. Christ, if I'm not in you in ten seconds, I'm going to come all over myself like an untrained teenager." Her giggle had him looking up. "Oh you think this is funny, do you? Wait, love. I'm going to have you begging for release before I'm finished with you."

Willow was suddenly on her back on the bed. Jared was leaning over her on his elbow. Her bra was gone and so was his shirt. She could feel the hair on his legs tickle her own.

"You're so beautiful." He moved the hair from her face as he spoke. "More beautiful every time I look at you."

"Take me, Jared. Please. Take me." he took them both.

~*Chapter 16*~

Jared woke when she came back to bed. She was cold as he pulled her back into his arms, but soon warmed up. He thought she had gone to let the dogs out. Next time, he told himself, next time he would do it. Her even breathing and a soft snore told him she had fallen back to sleep.

They had made love and she promptly fell asleep. Jared shifted his body to look down at her. Relaxed in her slumber, she took his breath away. Kissing her lightly on the lips, he went into her bath and after closing the door, looked at himself.

He had to grin. This reflection was much different than the one he'd first seen in the mirror after making love to her. This man looked happy, thrilled, and in love. After he disposed of the condom and cleaned up, he went back to the bed. She immediately wrapped around him.

Jared was going to tell her in the morning about who he was. His conversation with his father had told him a great deal about the woman in his arms. And there was something she needed to be made aware of. Things with Talbor had gotten out of hand.

The charges against the man stemming from the beating to death of a nineteen-year-old girl were just one of many. The police were also looking at him in a couple of other things as well. Jared didn't want Willow alone anymore. If Talbor was as nuts as the reports were saying, then he'd let nothing stand in his way to get to Willow.

Drifting asleep, he was pleased when she stayed wrapped around him. Sleeping with Willow and waking up next to her could become a very nice habit.

The noise in the hall woke him. It was still dark in the room, but he could see well enough to see the door. He reached for Willow and really wasn't surprised when her side of the bed was empty. Cursing, he got up and went to the door. The first thing he heard were the nails of the dogs clicking on the floor, next were voices.

Opening the door just a crack, he saw Willow and a man standing outside the other door down the hall. They were both coming out and she pulled something out of her pocket and he assumed, locked the door. They both went down the stairs with the dogs fast on their heels. He closed the door.

She was meeting a man? Why? He knew the man hadn't been her lover...not before now anyway. Leaning back against the door, he tried to think. Then in a fit of jealously, he opened the door and walked down the hall. Yes, it was locked. Going back to the room, he got into bed. He couldn't even figure out why he was so angry. He was going to wait for her to tell him.

When he woke the next time, the room was pink with the rising sun. Her side of the bed was still empty. He staggered to the shower and took a very quick one. It was just after seven and if he was going to get to work on time, he needed to hustle. He was slightly pissed about her not being there twice, but thought they were both getting used to sleeping together and maybe she'd been nervous. He walked into the kitchen and came to an abrupt halt. The man from the lot was standing in the kitchen with her. And they were both pissed.

"...don't give a good fuck what you want. I told you to not do it anymore. What the fuck is—" The man stopped when he saw Jared. "Who the fuck are you?"

Jared walked over to the counter and kissed Willow full on the mouth. He knew what it looked like. Like he was staking claim. Well, he was.

"None of your business" Willow told him calmly. "I want you out of my house right now. I've had it up to my ass in people telling me what to do."

The man looked over at Jared. "And he stays, I suppose? No, don't think so. You need a fucking...are you sleeping with him?"

The man's voice raised a few octaves when he'd asked. Jared wanted to hear what Willow told the man. And he wanted to know who he was. Marta shoved him and the man into a chair.

"You know you ain't gonna get no where's telling her what she is to do." The man started to rise. "Sit. Willow James, you introduce these two before they get blood all over my nice clean kitchen."

Willow huffed. "Not that it's any of either of your business, but Jared Robert, meet my asshole brother Alexander James. Alexander, meet my...met..."

"Her lover," Jared finished for her. Marta cackled behind them and set a huge platter of food on the table between them.

"You know how to stir up the pot, don't you, boy?" she told him with a wink. "Alexander, you eat now. You're momma is gonna have your hide coming in here demanding things from your sister like you done. Might be your last meal."

"And what do you think she's going to say when she finds out that her 'lover' is having breakfast here? You think she'll be thrilled about that?" Alexander picked up the platter and took half the bacon, sausage, and ham off it and handed it to Jared. "And Dad. What do you think he's going to say?"

Jared started to hand the platter to Willow, but she shook her head. Marta set an empty plate in front of her and Jared put some of the meat on the plate. Willow glared at him then turned on her brother.

"Oh grow up. What are you going to do, tell him? If you do, so help me I will tell him every little secret I know about you, including the night with Shelly Markus." Jared burst out laughing at the look on Alexander's face.

"You wouldn't dare. You said you'd take that to your grave, Wills. You wound me. I never thought I'd—"

Willow snorted and leaned back when a platter of eggs was laid on the table. There had to have been over a dozen of them. Jared watched as Alexander took five and handed the platter to him again. Jared just looked at him.

"You know you should serve women first, don't you? Not take what you want then hand it to someone else."

Now Alexander snorted as he dug into his breakfast. "If you hand the platter to her first, you might as well figure on being hungry. She can eat more than most men I know. Take what you want now and she can get more later. If you hang around her much, you'll see what I mean."

Willow murmured under her breath and Jared thought she said, "fucking prick," but wasn't sure. Whatever it had been, Marta apparently heard and smacked her on the hand with a spatula. Jared was thoroughly enjoying himself.

"If you don't mind my asking, what were you trying to get your sister to do that she won't?" Jared watched as another platter of food was set on the table and a plate of rolls. This time, Willow beat her brother.

"Ah come on, Wills. Give me at least one of them." Alexander looked at him. "Best sticky buns in the world. I want her to go home. This thing with that Tal—fuck, that hurt, Wills."

"And I'll kick you again if you don't shut up. I'm not going home. This is my home." She stood up and so did he. "I'm going to work. I'll see you both later and I mean it, Alexander. Not. One. Word."

She kissed him on the mouth and breezed out the door, taking the dogs out with her. He could hear them barking as they enjoyed the freedom.

Jared looked at Alexander. "You were saying?"

~o0o~

Willow heard the vehicles start to arrive. She was just getting the last of the invoices entered when the door opened. Conley came in first then Jared. She ignored them both, well, as much as she could. Both of them were big men. And neither of them looked happy.

"You know, I'm pretty sure that both of you have work to do. Why don't you get to it?" She wasn't surprised when they didn't leave. "I'll dock your wages if you don't get out of here."

The police were on their way and she didn't want them in the office when they arrived. Talbor had killed a young girl and they wanted to come by and talk to her. She was nervous enough without these two being here. Jared sat down and Conley leaned against the cabinet.

"Okay, but you have to leave soon. I have…someone is coming and I'm pretty sure that you two aren't invited." She tried to concentrate on her work, but they were driving her nuts.

Finally, at ten till eight, she went out the door and left them on their own. She had a lot to deal with today. And they were coming up on the finishing of a project. She was just starting to assign tasks when the police rolled up. No lights, but two men got out. And thankfully, Talbor wasn't there.

"I need a volunteer to get the glazing done in the main office and someone to do a plug check." Sherman raised his hand. "Okay, I want a count on the ones that need changing and the total we have completed."

The first officer walked toward her and Jared as suddenly in front of him. After what seemed an eternity, they both came toward her.

"Hey, boss? You doing something we should know about?" someone asked from the group, and she laughed. The officer stepped up beside her while Jared went into the building with the other cop.

"First of all, your foreman here isn't in any trouble, but one of the men you work with might be. We want to know if any of you have any knowledge of the whereabouts of Shawn Talbor, Jr. He's wanted for questioning."

No one said a word and Willow wasn't surprised. These men were a tight group and they wouldn't say anything without more information. Willow stepped forward.

"If any of you see him or talk to him, I need for you to let me know. At this point, from what I understand, the police just want to talk to him. Anything you guys know, please let the police know."

No one had any information, but all of them promised to keep an eye out. When the police left, Willow went to the second floor and began priming the walls for paint.

She pulled out the Shop Vac and began sweeping the dust off the walls. The mask she wore and the vacuum kept her from hearing anything and that was fine with her. She had a lot to think about.

The vacuum had a bagger on it because the dust from the drywall had to be bagged according to HEPA regulations. Then she got out the sprayer to apply the fast drying PVA or polyvinyl acetate drywall primer. After that it was just a matter of going back and forth with the sprayer in slow, even strokes.

She was in love with Jared. That part didn't bother her. It was the consequences that did. After this gig was up, she wouldn't see him again and she knew that. Not that he'd ever said anything…other than the tat, but she wasn't stupid.

Then there was the email she'd gotten from her parents. They were coming Friday. They said they were coming for an extended visit and that they wanted to talk to her about the hotelier job. And her mom had hinted that she would like to meet the man who they'd spoken of the other night and where they were in their relationship.

Relationship. Did they have one? Probably, she supposed, but not much of one. She knew nothing about him other than he worked hard and played harder. He made her laugh and he made her smile. Then there was the sex. Marta had been right; Jared did know his way around a body.

Thinking about last night, she shivered at what they had done, what he'd done to her and she to him. There wasn't an inch on her bed that they hadn't touched or used. When he'd said they were going to have fun, he hadn't been kidding. Then they got to use the bottom of the bed.

She'd gotten up to use the bathroom and when she came back, he was standing at the end of her bed waiting. Her pussy gushed for him when he motioned for her to come to him. When he got there, he had her stand in front of him and he turned her toward the far wall. There was a mirror there and he'd turned it so that they could see each other.

"See what you look like to me?" his hands cupped her breasts and he nipped her neck. "Watch us. I want you to see us together."

As his darker hands traced over her pale skin, she could feel his cock in her back. When he shifted and his cock was between the cleft of her legs, she watched as his cock head would peak through every time he rocked. For every one of his thrusts against her, she would rock back toward him.

"Jared, please, I want to come. I need to come." His hand trailed down her belly and she knew he was going to touch her. Excitement made her shaky and she spread her legs wider for him.

"That's it, baby. Let me touch you. I want you to watch you come." His fingers found her clit immediately and she rode his fingers. Over and over he pressed against her until she couldn't stand it. Begging him, she nearly cried out when he pushed her head down on the bed.

"Look, Willow. Look in the mirror when I fuck you." She turned her head toward the mirror again and watched as he held his cock with one hand and gripped her hip with the other.

Slowly, he had entered an inch in and then out. She watched as his cock became slick with her juices. When he was seated in as deep as he could go, she felt his other hand grab her hip and he started to fuck her harder, then harder still. And they both watched every time his cock made her breasts bounce, every time his balls slapped against her ass.

Reaching around to her pussy, she felt him tug and press at her clit. The pressure was building and she knew it was just a matter of seconds before she shattered. His body leaning over hers, his weight bearing her down, she felt him bite her shoulder. It sent her into the stratosphere. When he pulled out of her and flipped her onto her back, she wasn't sure what he was going to do, but when he lifted her legs and put them over his shoulders, she nearly cried out when he slammed into her again. She was tighter this way, his cock deeper.

"Come, baby. Come now and tighten that delicious pussy over me. Fuck, Willow, I'm coming."

Her legs suddenly spread and he was over her. His cock hit her clit with every stroke as he roared out his release. As soon as she came again, she felt him drop onto her and she knew that she was finished. Slipping into a deep sleep, Willow knew that this bed was the best thing she'd ever bought.

Someone pecking on her shoulder made her jerk around. She had been so caught up in the memory she'd completely forgotten what she'd been doing. Looking at the wall, she was happy to see that her mind was on her work at least. She took off the mask to look at Jared. He was grinning.

"Your face is all flushed and your nipples are hard. Would you like to share with me what you were thinking about?"

She felt her face heat up more. "No, I would not. What do you want? I've got a lot to do."

"You know you say that to me a lot. It's noon." He stepped back as he spoke to show her the lunch he'd set up. "Aren't you hungry? Marta packed us a big lunch. She said something about you needing more calories."

After lunch, she continued to work on the walls. She would have someone come and check about something off and on, but for the most part, she was left alone. It suited her mood and she thought maybe everyone knew it. By six, she was ready to go home.

~Chapter 17~

At midnight, Shawn was back at the site. There was no one around, but he'd counted eight cruiser drive-bys in the last two hours. He blamed the bitch for it and pulled out his little notebook and wrote that down too. There was plenty she had to pay for and he was keeping track.

When the next cruiser drove by, he made his way to the trailer. At the rate he was going, he'd still be trying to get there when everyone showed up in the morning. Shawn was hiding near the steps when another car drove by, this one a regular car. He took out the keys, unlocked the door, and stepped inside.

Getting a set of if site keys had been brilliant, he thought. He knew where all the people lived, of course, and it hadn't been any problem getting into the house of Conley. It was after Conley had shown up that the problems had begun. Had he just turned over the keys when he'd asked politely, then he wouldn't have had to rough up his missus. Course that didn't help good ol' boy Conley much, but that was the way things went down.

Shawn laughed when he thought about how he'd tussled them both up and left them. They'd be dead by morning anyway so it didn't matter much that he'd trashed the house not thinking about prints. He was on a mission.

He pulled out the desk drawers and dumped them. Nothing but papers. Damn it, where did she keep the fucking keys to the storage lot? He pulled out more paper from other drawers. There was nothing under the computer and he couldn't find anything in the chair he'd cut up either. Sitting down on the ruined desk chair, he pulled out his stash and took another hit of drugs.

"Ahhhh, now that's more like it." His body caught fire the moment the drugs hit his system. A euphoric feeling washed over him and he felt relaxed, more himself. He sat there for only a few seconds before he heard someone pounding on the door. Shawn got up and went to it.

"Who's there?" He thought he sounded normal, but the person on the other side pounded again. Louder now, he asked again.

"Police. Open up. And put your hands out where I can see them."

Shawn panicked. And when he panicked, he got stupid. He hated being stupid. Pulling out his gun, he tried to think what to do.

"Think, think, think," he ordered himself as he beat his head on the door. "There is only one way out of this and that's killing time."

Shawn turned around and pointed his gun at the voices he'd heard speaking. No one was there. It was her again, he just knew it. Putting the gun in the waistband of his pants, he pulled out the notebook again. Dropping it, he leaned over to get it and that's when the cop burst through the door.

Shawn fell forward and bobbled his gun. He didn't even hesitate when he scooped it up in his hands and turned it on the policeman. There was a split second when he had a single clear thought. This, he thought, this is going to be my crowning glory. He fired six times, hitting the cop twice in the belly and once in the leg, throwing him out of the doorway and out into the lot behind him.

Laughing hard and struggling to get up, Shawn followed the cop into the yard and watched with fascination as the cop tried to crawl away. Tiring of the show, Shawn picked up the cop's gun and shot him eight more times, each shot hitting him dead center in the heart.

He went back into the trailer and found his notebook he'd dropped. Finding a pen in the mess in the office supplies strewn about the room, he sat in the chair again and wrote.

"Caused me to kill a cop—punishment, one bullet to the head." Shawn looked at his list of transgressions that the bitch had to pay for and shook his head. "You are going to be one sorry bitch. Yeah, one sorry, sorry bitch."

~o0o~

Willow was in the kitchen with Marta when someone pulled in the driveway the next morning. At first she thought it was her parents, but when a man she didn't recognize stepped out, she was surprised. It was seven o'clock in the morning…on a Thursday. When he came to the door, she met him there.

"May I help you?" She looked at the car he drove and a very lovely woman stepped out as a driver opened the door for her. Willow looked back at the man.

"You must be Willow James. I'm J.R. Stone. I've heard a great deal about you." he looked back at the woman then back at Willow. "May I speak to my son? I'm sorry about the hour, but it's important. Something has come up and, well…you're going to have to hear it too, I'm afraid."

Willow was confused. She knew the man, but not his son and before she could say anything, she realized who he was. Grabbing onto the door, she nodded her head. "Jared Robert Stone is your son." She looked at the woman who was coming up the steps.

"Yes. I've tried the house, you see, and he's not…are you all right, my dear? You look a bit peaked."

The next thing she knew, she was seated in a chair with her head between her knees. The hurt wasn't any better from this position either. She tried to sit up twice and someone kept pushing her down. Finally, she'd had enough.

"Let me go. I'm…I'm fine." No she wasn't and she had a feeling she never would be again. "I'll go and get your son. He's…he's here."

The woman blocked her path before she could make her escape. "He didn't tell you, did he?"

Willow shook her head and moved out of the room. She hoped that Marta would take care of them. Willow's mother would never forgive her if she was a poor host. Giggling uncontrollably, she rounded the stairs for now and went to find the dogs. They were sleeping in the family room.

She sat there for several minutes just looking at them. She didn't know what she'd been thinking in that time. She'd actually been trying not to. Finally knowing she had to do it, she went to her bedroom to wake Jared.

He was sleeping so soundly. They'd made love most of the night and talked the rest. She'd told him things she'd never told anyone before. And now…well, she wasn't sure what would happen now.

She leaned over and shook his leg. He didn't move. He just wasn't a morning person, he'd told her. This time, she grabbed the blanket and tore it off him.

"Hey," he said, coming awake quickly. "That's no way to wake a man. Come here and make it up to me." When he reached for her, she stepped back.

"Your father is downstairs. He needs to talk to you about something." She stepped back more when he leapt from the bed. "Your mom is down there too."

"Christ." He yanked on his pants. "Did he say what it was about? And my mom too? Must be bad if he brought…"

She could see the moment that it hit him that she knew. With his pants up but yet to be zipped, he turned to her. He looked at her for long moments before he spoke. "I was going to tell you last night. But I got distracted. It's not what it looks like and whatever you're thinking, it's not that either."

He sounded mad. Well, so was she. "And what is it supposed to be like, Jared? Tell me. Does it look like you've been fucking the help? Were you here to check up on the news you've been getting from Talbor and decided to get laid while you were here?" His flush told her she'd guessed. "Oh my God. You did, didn't you?"

She started to turn away when he stopped her by grabbing her arm. "What about you, Willow? Rich girl working as a laborer on a construction site? For what? Shits and giggles? And what about your secrets? Huh, want to tell them to me?"

"What the fuck are you talking about? I don't have any secrets."

He grabbed her arm and pulled her from the room. When they were before the spare bedroom, he pointed to it.

"What's in there? You keep it locked all the time. What do you have hidden in there?"

Willow thought she'd been hurt before, but nothing prepared her for what it felt like to have not only her heart ripped from her chest, but her trust too. Reaching above the door, she took the key and handed it to him. He looked confused.

"Open it. Go ahead. We're baring our souls here. Open it." When he continued to stand there, she took the key from his hand and shoved it into the lock. She heard him say her name, but she ignored him. She threw the door back with a bang. "You'll have to forgive me for not sharing this with you. You see, this wasn't a secret so much as something I didn't think to share." her voice cracked and she had to take a deep breath.

Jared stepped into the room. "What is this?"

What did she tell him? Then she remembered his parents where downstairs in her kitchen and she didn't care anymore.

"They're donations. I gather things throughout the year and I take them to shelters and other charities that don't seem to have enough money to get the supplies they need to get by." She looked at the room through his eyes. "The toys are marked by age and sex. I take those to the orphanage twice a year or sooner if they need them. The other things, the wipes and diapers, are there when someone needs them. They come by when they run low and I replenish them here. There you have it, my big secret. I buy toys for children and I have a stash of diapers."

He turned to her then. "The other night, a man was here. You were coming out of this room."

She remembered. Joel had come because someone had had a house fire and their baby was without supplies. She'd helped him pack his car. And Jared had seen her. She wondered what he'd thought then. He'd thought the worst, no doubt. If he hadn't, he would have come to her about it.

Willow wondered if she could hurt any more. When Jared turned back to the room, Willow went to the stairs. It was too much.

She had to go through the kitchen because her jacket and keys were there, but she didn't want to speak to anyone. Marta handed her her jacket as she swept through, and her wallet. Kissing her on the cheek, Willow turned to Mr. and Mrs. Stone. "He's coming down. I don't think he'll be much longer." She turned to Marta. "Could you see to the dogs for me?" At her nod, Willow left.

It was well after ten in the morning when she realized she needed to stop somewhere. Her truck was on empty and she thought she might be as well. Giggling slightly, she pulled into the gas station and began filling up.

He'd been playing her all along. Tears threatened again and she had to fight hard not to cry in public. Trying to think about anything else, she finished filling up and went inside to get something to eat and drink. Willow couldn't go long without food. Her overactive metabolism had already burned through the dinner she'd had last night. Grabbing several candy bars and three bottles of water, she went back to her truck.

When her phone vibrated off the seat, she reached for it. The icons across the top were all about messages—email, texting and voice mail. She scrolled through the phone log and saw that most of the calls were from her house and quite a few more were from the site. There was one from Conley and two from her mother. She called her mom.

"Hello, darling. I was wondering if you wouldn't mind if we came tonight instead of tomorrow? Your father has it in his head that a storm will keep us from getting there in one piece."

She looked out the window of her truck and saw that a storm did look like it was in the making. Dark clouds were over the South and she wondered what the temperature was.

"Sure. I might not be...you're already on your way, aren't you? How close are you or are you already here?" Willow closed her eyes against the thought of her mom and dad hearing about Jared.

"You always have been too perceptive. We got here an hour ago. We're staying at the one on Wilshire Boulevard. Can you meet us here after you get off work?"

Work. She'd forgotten about work. Not that she could work there anymore not with Jared...her mom was speaking.

"...call him. He said that you need to pick up your phone. Oh and he'll be coming to dinner with us too. I hope you don't mind, but we haven't seen him since the two of you came up that weekend."

Her brother. For a minute there she'd thought her mother was speaking of Jared, but realized that he'd never met them before. But he had met Alexander. Willow wondered if they had exchanged numbers and that's why he wanted her to call. Willow realized that the conversation had died or she'd lost connection.

"Mom?"

"Yes, dear. What's happened? Have you had a fight with that boy?"

Willow couldn't lie to her, nor could she tell her the truth. How did she tell her mom that she'd slept with the owner's son and he'd been doing her...a lot to see if the information they'd gotten from one of her employees was correct.

"I have to go. I'm fine. I don't...I'll have to call you about dinner. I'm a little...I have to do some catch up work before I can make any plans." Willow hung up on her mom.

The next person she called was Alexander. And she was right, he did have Jared's number and vice versa. As soon as he answered the phone, he started in on her.

"Where the fuck are you? Damn it, Willow, we've been worried sick."

She hung up.

~Chapter 18~

Shawn hated his hotel room. It was cheap and ugly. But he felt that he could hide here in relative comfort. But he had to figure out how to get the merchandise back and get it back soon. The Voice wasn't going to wait any longer and he had until midnight to get it to him or Shawn was dead. He wondered if it was about time he had his dad come in and fix this. And he picked up his phone to do so.

The call couldn't be placed. He tried six different times to put it through and he got the same message each time. "Please call customer service if you are experiencing difficulty." he looked at the phone on the end table in his shitty hotel and realized he had no idea what his father's number was. His first call was to the cell phone company and he knew that number because the bitch kept telling him.

"I'm sorry, sir, but I can't give you that information without verification from the cell phone holder. If you can just get him to call, we can talk to him."

Shawn rubbed his eyes. He'd told this one twice now that he didn't know his father's phone number; they'd locked him out of it when their fucking phone stopped working.

"I can't call my dad. You have to do it or let me have my service back to call him. I don't write the fucking numbers down when I store them in my phone."

The voice on the other end was no longer professional. "If you use that language once more, Mr. Talbor, I will hang up on you and put a note in your—"

"You think I give a good fuck what you put in a note? Give me back my fucking service." he waited for her to say something to that. And waited. Then the dial tone sounded. She'd hung up on him. He started to dial the number again when he realized that someone was pounding on his door.

"Who is it? I'm busy here and I don't have time for shit today." Shawn wrenched open the door. "What?"

The man standing there looked like he'd just gotten up. His hair was mussed and his pajamas where rumpled. And he looked pissed.

"Do you think you can please keep it down? I realize that the walls are thin, but I think I would be able to hear you if we were on separate floors. I have an interview in the morning and I don't want to have to go in looking like I haven't slept in days."

He told Shawn this like he was supposed to give a shit. Before he could tell the guy what he could do with his thin walls and quiet time, he saw her. The bitch was going into one of the rooms across from him. He nearly went after her then, but he had to get rid of this shithole and plan. He simply punched the guy in the face.

"See if that will help with the quiet you fucking fuck-tard." The guy staggered back and Shawn slammed the door in his face.

She was here. He couldn't believe it, the bitch was right here, right now. He walked over to the bed and sat down. Shawn reached for the baggie of his own stash laying there and measured out himself a good hit. He didn't know why this shit was illegal; it certainly made him think better. He sat and waited for the rush to hit him and closed his eyes and lay back on the bed when it did.

If the bitch was here, she was meeting somebody. If she was meeting somebody, then there might be someone else in the room if he just went charging over there. He had to scope things out first.

Shawn got up off the bed, went to the window, and pulled back the curtain. She was in number seventeen and sure enough, that was her truck out front. He stood there watching and waiting when she came out and went to the truck again. He was about ready to go out and snatch her when she only got something out of her truck bed.

Shawn watched for another twenty minutes and no one showed up. He was ready to make his move. He made sure his gun was loaded and that he had his key. He'd have to take care that no one disturbed them because it was high time the bitch paid. He tried to think where to take her when he realized if she was here then the job site was empty. He'd take her there. He looked out the window again and saw a van pull up beside her.

Shawn was getting to the point where he wanted to go out and kill the fucking family of eleven-hundred that had pulled up beside her room. It wasn't really that many, he reminded himself. He'd counted. And he'd only come up with six of them, but damn, those people sure were taking their time getting settled, he thought, for the tenth time. How many trips to the vehicle did one family have to make for Christ's sake?

Finally. After an hour, he was ready to make his move. He moved across the hotel parking lot, keeping close to the walls, when he saw a car that made him nervous. The bitch had called The Voice, he just knew it. Hurrying now, he went back to his room and decided to wait.

~o0o~

Willow was checked into number seventeen again. She didn't want that room, but it was the only one left, the clerk had told her. She wanted to stay here in this hotel because it was familiar to her, but not in their room. She went inside first to see if it hurt too bad to be there. Then she went out and got her bag. She'd stay, but tomorrow she was going home. She missed the dogs and Marta. And no one was running her out of her house.

Her phone was on the charger now and when she came back into the room after grabbing some dinner, it was ringing. She knew by the tone it was Jared again, so she didn't even bother answering. As soon as it went to voicemail her phone rang again, this time her brother. She decided to give him another chance.

"If you say one word I don't like, I'm hanging up. I have a headache and I just want to be left alone. All right, Alexander?"

She wasn't sure he was going to answer her and she couldn't make herself care right now. Just when she was going to hang up, he answered her.

"Yes, but let me say that he's sorry for what he did."

"He lied to me. And if you think that's okay between lovers, then I'm not sure I like you all that much right now either." She sat on the bed and listened to the people next door get settled. "He hurt me. And he lied. I'm sorry if I don't find that to be all that comforting right now."

He was quiet for a few seconds and she could hear mumbling. She knew who was with him; she knew his voice as well as her own. Jared was wherever Alexander was. She strained to hear, but she couldn't make anything out.

"He wants to know if you'll talk to him. He said there are things going on that you need to be made aware of and he's worried for your safety." Alexander lowered his voice. "I think you should do it, Wills. There's been a murder."

Willow knew about the murder at the site. It had been all over the news since early morning. She also knew who they suspected. It didn't surprise her that Talbor was considered armed and dangerous. He'd been threatening her for weeks. Willow did feel terrible about the policeman who'd been killed, and the girl too. The cop had only been doing his job and nobody deserved to die like that. And the girl...to murder someone in front of people in your own home...well, that was just sick.

"Alexander, do you have any idea what he did? What he didn't tell me?" When he didn't answer her, she went on. "Alexander, I love him. What am I supposed to do with that?"

"Talk to him. Tell him." The next voice she heard was Jared's. Apparently. Alexander didn't want her to say no. "Are you all right?" She didn't answer; the tears were threatening to come again. "You're parents are here...so are mine. None of them are very happy with me right now. Well, neither am I. Happy with myself, I mean."

"I don't—" Someone was pounding on her door and when she went to the peep hole, there was no one there. "Hang on a minute, this door sticks and I have to use two hands."

She was stalling. Willow knew if she didn't go to the door then whoever it was would simply go away. She just needed a few extra minutes. Willow set the phone on the dresser and pried the door open. She had just taken the lock off when she was thrown back and hit the bed behind her. Before she could get up and figure out what had happened, Talbor was on her.

His hand was over her mouth as she screamed. And when he bounced her head on the floor twice, she shut up. It was either that or have permanent brain damage. The gun under her chin bit deep into her skin.

"Now you listen here you bitch. This is what we're going to do. You're going to answer some questions, and I'm going to ask them. You understand?"

No! She wanted to scream at him, but was afraid to move. He had his knees in her ribs and his other hand not holding the gun around her throat. She was beginning to see spots before her eyes and she was afraid if she fell unconscious, he'd kill her for spite. Her head hit the floor again.

"You fucking hear me, cunt? I'm going to answer some questions and you're going to...no, damn it." He moved the gun and before she could breathe, he backhanded her with the gun. "You fucking bitch. You're confusing me. I will ask you questions and you will answer them."

She could feel the blood trickle down her cheek and her entire face felt as if it had exploded. Not moving, she watched him sit on her chest and pull out a bloodied notepad. He took out a broken pencil and began writing in it. Willow couldn't understand all of what he was saying, but it sounded like he was saying she was going to be punished for making him slap her. She sat up and tried to knock him off her.

The pen and pad went one way and he the other. It took everything she had to roll over him and try to get to the door. The gun wasn't anywhere she could see it and she decided that she didn't know how to use it anyway. She grabbed the door handle when he smashed her head against the door frame. She felt her head open and blood pour from her forehead. Her scream was cut off by him yanking her around to face him and his fist connecting soundly with her cheek. A moment of pain, intense pain, and that was it.

~Chapter 19~

Jared dropped to the floor the moment she screamed. He could hear the scuffle going on and started screaming for her. He knew the man who had her and he was hurting her. Willow's father took the phone from him before he could say anything. When he paled too, Jared knew that it wasn't good.

He sat down hard on the chair and looked at Jared. Edgar gently laid the phone on the table and reached for his wife. Before Jared could ask, Edgar shook his head.

"I need a moment. Call the police. He has her, he has Willow. I heard...I heard him...he hit her. The bastard hit my little girl." Willow's mom, Amanda, and Jared's mom held each other. In the hours they'd been trying to find Willow, the two older women had formed a bond.

While they waited on the police and the special unit that Edgar had brought in to help, Jared thought about the day. Since he'd come downstairs and found his parents in the kitchen and Willow gone it had been one roller coaster ride after another. First, the fight he'd had with his mom.

"You didn't tell her. After sleeping with her, you didn't tell her who you were. Jared Robert Stone, if you weren't over six feet tall, I'd beat your ass. How could you?" He started to say something, but thought better of it. His dad, however, didn't have any problems.

"You should be horse whipped. That poor girl looked like I pole axed her. Nearly passed out on us. What do you have to say for yourself, young man?"

Jared sat down. "Nothing, sir. I meant to tell her last night, but I got…we… Nothing, sir, I should have told her."

Jared felt ten years old. He was a grown man and his parents were disappointed in him. Hell, he was disappointed in him. He looked over at his mom.

"I love her." Marta snorted and he turned to her. "I do. I know I don't have any excuses for what I did, but I do love her."

"Well 'bout time one of you said it. Dumb kids now days. Course you love her, and she loves you too. Both of you too wrapped up in getting into each other pants to see it." Marta set a platter of food in front of him. "Eat. You need your strength. I called her momma and daddy. They on their way. That brother of hers too, Alexander. Don't you be surprised none if he knocks you on your ass a couple of times either."

And he had. Alexander came into the door and socked him right in the mouth. His parents had been shocked, then his mom started laughing. He didn't see the humor in it, but apparently his dad did too. He decided to sit where he was until someone listened to his side. Marta handed him a baggie of ice and a stern look. Jared put the icepack on his mouth and didn't say much unless asked.

Jared didn't really have any delusion about what he'd done. He'd fucked up. He knew he should have told her who he was from the beginning, but didn't want to spoil what they had. Then when he'd discovered he had fallen in love with her, he'd thought, stupidly, he now realized, that he would make her fall in love with him before he told her.

When her parents had arrived twenty minutes later, her mom wouldn't even look at him. Jared figured she had spoken to Alexander. Willow's dad went outside in the light snow and played with the dogs for a while. Jared suspected he was trying to curb his temper. Jared knew he would be. When he came inside, he took Jared to Willow's office, another room he'd not been in.

It was a huge room and bright in the late afternoon sun. The wall that faced the wooded area out back had a door that opened out onto a private deck. The door was surrounded on both sides by large glass panels that were as big as the door but done in leaded glass panels and a stained glass mural over the three of them. The picture in glass depicted an orchard with the trees heavy with fruit and pickers with a truck and tractor full of baskets.

The walls on either side of the glass door were shelves were filled with books. Paperback and hard backs, romance and science, there were even a few texted books in amongst them. Jared himself was an eclectic reader and was happy to see that she was too.

The fourth wall was covered in pictures. Photographs and drawings fought for space on the huge wall. The only free space was the massive fireplace that had the biggest mantle he'd ever seen. Carved stone, it was at least seven feet long, ten inches thick, and it had to be, at the very minimum, fifteen inches wide. It too was covered in photos, as well as crowned with snowmen.

They were as varied as her book collection. Stuffed, ceramic, tall and short, there were hanging ones and standing ones as well as several sitting in a row all together around a basket of what appeared to be hundreds of small ornaments ready to hang on a tree, all snowmen in every color of the rainbow and patterns of material known to man. Jared walked over, picked up one from the basket, and held it up.

"She gets those as gifts every year from the homeless shelter. They try to outdo the year before. Wills must have over a thousand of those ugly things. She's fixing up one of the rooms here to hold them all." Edgar looked around the room before he sat down. "This isn't even a drop in the hat of what she has. She's been collecting them since she was a kid. Snowmen, of all things." Edgar shook his head, pride in his voice.

Jared sat down next to the man. Neither man sat in the chair behind the desk, knowing that they didn't belong there, Jared assumed. He waited until the man looked at him before he spoke.

"I love her. I know that I hurt her, but I do love her. And if she'll have me back, I'm going to marry her." As soon as the words were out of his mouth, he knew it was true. He wanted Willow for his wife.

"She's my baby girl. And you hurt what's mine. And in my book, that makes you responsible for her being gone." Edgar looked at him for several seconds before he continued. "I'm a fair man, a good man, I think. So, just so we're clear, if she doesn't forgive you, I'm having you killed." Edgar got up from the seat and left Jared sitting there.

That had been several hours ago and they had since formed a sort of truce. Then this happened. Willow had been kidnapped and he knew it was his fault.

There were all in the living room now. No one was saying much, but it was obvious they were worried and upset. Jared looked over at Amanda when she sat next to him on the big sofa. He was sure she was going to ask him to leave.

"Your parents are very nice, Jared. I like them." Jared looked over at them when she did. "You look a great deal like your father."

Jared had been told that before. He only wished he was as good a man as his father—both his parents really. They were what his grandda had called good peoples.

"Yes, ma'am, they are. They're the best." He looked at her now. "I'm sorry, Mrs. James. I never meant to hurt Willow. And I will never forgive myself because she's hurt. I love her very much. I want you to believe that."

Of course I do. You're not responsible for that lunatic taking her. He is a sick individual and should have been shot a good many years ago. Your mother tells me he has been that way since childhood."

Jared nodded. "Yes, ma'am. But I should have—"

"Do you think in all the years we've been married that I haven't hurt Edgar or that he hasn't hurt me? We both have, and sometimes on purpose. You should have done just what you did. I have to tell you, Willow can be a tad stubborn. She gets that from her father." Amanda smiled. "Me too, if truth be known. But if you tell, I'll deny that I said that. And I know Willow loves you. She would never have given you her virginity if she hadn't."

Jared felt the world tilt on its axis. He was both embarrassed and surprised by her bluntness. Before he could make any sort of reply, Alexander came rushing into the room.

"They found her truck. It's at the Starbright Hotel on Broad Street. The FBI are there now."

Not only did Jared's world tilt again, but this time it rotated a whole three-hundred-sixty degrees. She'd been at their hotel.

~oOo~

Willow woke slowly then wished that she hadn't. Every part of her body hurt. Some places hurt that she didn't even know she had until then. She tried to move, but found she was tied up. That's when she remembered Talbor.

She couldn't see much. It was dark and things wouldn't come into focus well. Every time she tried to grasp what she was seeing, sharp pains exploded in her brain. A flare of light hit her in the face and she wrenched back from it only to cause herself more pain. A moan spilled from her mouth.

"'Bout time you woke up. You think I got all day to wait on you during your nappy time? I have things I gotta take care of."

Talbor stood over her, shining the light in her face. When he shone it around the room, she could make out objects now and it took her several seconds to realize they were at the job site. They were on the third floor. She knew this because they had moved all the equipment up there to make sure that no one could take it before it was to be moved to the storage lot. Looking down, she could see that he had put bungee cords around her wrists and ankles and they were biting into her skin.

"Don't try anything stupid or I'll kill you." He made a production of showing her the knife he had in his hand. "I want them keys. Give 'em to me and I'll kill you real quick."

Keys? She didn't know what he was talking about and couldn't answer him anyway. The gag in her mouth prevented her from asking him. But he either thought she could speak telepathically or around the fucking rag because he came at her again.

"Fucking bitch." A kick to her ribs made her see stars. "When I ask you something, you'd better fucking answer."

This time, he kicked her twice in the ribs then once more in the belly. Crying now, she felt her ribs were broken with every breath she took.

Flashing the light over her, he stopped at her face. "Oh fuck, I tied your mouth up. Your fault. Yep, all your fault too. You were moaning everything I had to pick you up so I had to do something to shut you the fuck up. You're a heavy bitch, ain't cha?"

He jerked the rag from her mouth and tore her lips open again. She rubbed her cheek on her shoulder and screamed out at the pain it caused her. She started sobbing again.

"You keep that up and I'll gag you again. And don't think 'cause I lost my notebook don't mean I don't remember what you've done." He crouched down to her level. "Give me the keys. I only got an hour and time is money."

"What…what keys?" Her mouth hurt to speak. "I don't know—"

The pain hit her leg so quickly she screamed again. Which earned her another slap. She couldn't even see what he'd done, but his next works sent a chill down her body.

"You made me lose my gun so I had to improvise." he held the flashlight on his "gun." "Yep, nice and handy, this here."

The air compressor nail gun they used fit in his hand; the air hoses that had been put into each room had been coiled up and put in this room too. He must have gotten some of them out and hooked the compressor up to it while she'd been out.

The second nail made her sick. She was sobbing now from the pain and was afraid she would pass out. She was sure if she did, he'd kill her.

She couldn't even speak to him now, not even after he kicked her several more times. It wasn't until she saw the other man that she realized that she must have passed out.

Talbor had dropped the gun next to her in his haste to see the other man.

"It was all her fault. That stupid bitch, it's all her fault." Talbor pointed at her.

Willow tried to focus, but simply let the pain take her away. Her last thought was that she was going to die and she hadn't told Jared she loved him.

~Chapter 20~

Daniel looked at the woman on the floor in a pool of her own blood. He stepped toward her and with a flick of his gun, Talbor backed away. Daniel leaned down and felt for a pulse. Weak. She'd be lucky if she made it to sunrise. If he was inclined to let her live that long. Which he most certainly was not going to do.

"She did this. It's all her fault that I don't have your drugs. I—"

Daniel shot him in the gut. Talbor went down quickly and started screaming. Daniel wasn't in the mood and walked over to the man to couch down to him. "Shut up or die." his voice was calm; it was something Daniel had worked very hard on. Not showing his anger in his voice. It worked too, most of the time. He put the gun in Talbor's mouth. That worked wonders, too, at shutting him up.

"Now, you and I are going to have a conversation about my merchandise." Daniel enunciated each syllable so that Talbor would understand that the "D" word was not to be used. "What are you going to tell me about the girl over there and her involvement?"

If Willow James was involved then not only was she dead, but her family as well. The powers over his head were demanding that he make everyone aware of him being in charge now. Daniel didn't care so long as nothing came back on him. He pulled the gun out enough so that Talbor could speak.

"She hid the keys from me. Wouldn't give 'em to me even when I asked her real nice like. You can see what I had to do. That's all on her. You gonna call me an ambulance? I think I'm hurt real bad."

Daniel ignored the request. There was no way this man was going to be going to the hospital. And if he did, it would be in a long black bag in the back of the coroner wagon.

"Did she know about my merchandise? And if you lie to me, I'll shoot your fucking dick off." Daniel laughed when Talbor cover his dick with his bloodied hands. Like that would stop him.

"She didn't know about the dru…merchandise. But she's been fucking with me since I hid them. And she slept with every one of them cocksuckers that works for her but me."

Daniel looked over at the girl. She was going to die because she had the good sense not to sleep with Talbor. He shook his head and turned back to Talbor.

There was no way Daniel could get to his merchandise now. He was sure that the place was being watched at the lot. Hell, this fool had killed a cop here not twenty-four hours ago. He was glad that he had men he could trust keeping an eye on things while he was here taking care of business. Now all that was left was to take care of this loose end. Well, now there were two counting the woman.

"You've reached the limit of your usefulness Talbor. And I'm not so sure why you were hired in the first place, to be honest. If I hadn't already killed my predecessor, I'd hunt him down and do it again for having the stupid nerve to hire you in the first place." The silencer made the shot to Talbor's head sound like a soft pop. "You cost me much more than—"

The shot knocked him over Talbor and onto the floor on the other side of him. Pain exploded in his back as he dropped the gun and flashlight. He couldn't see shit now and tried to remain as still as possible, thinking if he couldn't see them, then they couldn't see him either.

Daniel cried out when the second shot hit him in the knee. He felt it shatter from the impact. The blood running down his leg was making the floor slick beneath him and he was having a hard time trying to get away from whoever it was.

He couldn't think where the fuck his men were. They were supposed to back him up and warn him when someone showed up. He kept searching for the light or the gun when he wrapped his hands around the handle of something. The flashlight. He held it up and had to bang it twice in his hand before it flared to life again.

"Mother fuck." The girl was pointing the nail gun at him. Her eyes were closed and he thought maybe she had finally passed out or was dead. Either way, the fucking bitch was going to pay for this.

He couldn't stand. The nails, he knew what they were now, had hurt him badly. He dragged himself over to a stack of drywall and tried to get his good foot under him. The third nail caught him in the shoulder and knocked him back a bit. He was in agony and he was starting to get dizzy. Looking down, he could see a good bit of the nail in his knee still sticking out and that made his belly roll. She was going to pay.

The nail gun lay in both her hands and rested on the floor. Her eyes were closed again, but there was no way he was going to take the chance of her being passed out. He wondered how she could even see him with her face swollen like it was.

There was also a large cut on her forehead that he'd noticed earlier and her lips were cut and bleeding. By all rights, the fucking bitch should have been dead by now. He wondered how she could see him when he realized the moon was shining directly behind him, making him a perfect target for her.

Using the light, he searched for the gun. He wasn't going to fuck with her any longer. As soon as he wrapped his fingers around the butt, another nail hit him in the belly. He covered his hand with it only to discover no nail protruded from this wound. It had gone through and through.

Daniel couldn't lift his right arm, and he knew he couldn't fire worth shit with his left. But he knew she had a near endless supply of nails and he was losing blood fast. He was already feeling weak.

"I'm going to hunt your family down, Willow James. I'm going to kill them all slowly if you don't put that fucking gun down now." he struggled to stand again. "Then I'm going to laugh my ass off. Do you want to know why, Willow? Because I win."

Standing now, but leaning heavily on the stack, he lifted the gun and aimed at her the second she lifted the air gun. He felt the impact immediately and the glass shattered behind him.

The nail had entered his throat and tore into him. He was falling backwards and because of the blood at his feet, he couldn't seem to get a purchase as he went through the large window behind him. Glass cut into his back and legs as he broke through it. As soon as he hit the ground below, he knew something was wrong.

Pain ricocheted through his head, but strangely, not the rest of his body. He couldn't move, couldn't lift his arms, wiggle his toes. Blood touched his face. It was warm and that was all he could feel.

Seconds, no more than that, passed and one of his men stood over him. Daniel heard him say "fuck" then he disappeared. Daniel wanted to call him back, to beg him to call for help, but he couldn't move, couldn't speak. He was beginning to feel lightheaded and cold. Things were fading; his vision blurred. He looked up at the window where he'd fallen and realized that he'd broken his back. His last thought was that the bitch was going to pay for this. He was going to make his own list.

~oOo~

J.R. held his wife and watched his son pace the room. It had been over seventeen hours since J.R. had come to this house and a little less than five since Willow had come up missing. Then there was the issue with Thomas Conley and his family. He'd been found late last night. He and his wife had taken quite a beating and were lucky that one of their children had found them when he had. While in critical condition, both adults would make a full recovery.

J.R. was startled out of his thoughts when Edgar spoke softly to him. He, too, held his sleeping wife.

"Do you think they'll find her soon? My baby's been with that bastard a long time. Maybe they've taken her out of the state." J.R. didn't miss that Edgar hadn't mentioned that he could be hurting her again.

The police had found the notebook at the hotel. They figured it belonged to Shawn. And they had confirmed that the blood on it and in the room had been Willow's. A person who J.R. had bribed had told him that it was filled with dates and names and that the few that the police had researched were dead. It looked as though Shawn had been keeping track of the people he'd been killing and how he'd done it. There were over fifty names in the book, including his own mother. But it was the back of the book that had sent chills down their spines.

He had a list of "punishments" that he felt Willow had coming to her. Some of the infractions in his eyes were as petty as her not taking a lunch break with him to her sleeping with everyone but him. It had been the hardest thing he'd ever done telling Jared and the James what he'd learned.

Edgar simply held his sobbing wife; Alexander left the house, while Jared gathered his coat without saying a word and took the dogs outside into the yard. Looking at his watch, J.R. realized that Jared had been out there for over two hours.

"I'm not sure, Edgar. I'd like to think she's here close to us. But you're right, he is a sick bastard."

Marta came into the room and looked at both of them. She looked worried and confused.

"The police is on the phone for you, Mr. Stone. Said they be a problem down at your site. Said if you got a silent alarm down there you'd best be bringing everybody down to see about it." J.R. looked at the woman, his own confusion evident. "Said you needed to know you have a scanner if anyone was to ask you how you come to be knowing about the incident. You got one of them in here?"

"Scanner? No, I don't—" Suddenly, he got it. "Shit! They've found her. Quick, get the boys. Hurry before someone calls and tells us not to come down."

"You don't worry none about them telling you that, sir. I got your back. Go get my girl and bring her back. I got her some sticky buns to eat." With that, Marta went to the kitchen.

In less than ten minutes, they were all piling into the limo. In another twenty, they were pulling into the site lot.

The place was alight with blue and red strobing lights and uniformed personnel. The yellow tape went around the entire building as well as the tape that had already gone around the site trailer. Looking up when he heard the whoop-whoop of helicopter blades, he saw two of them flying low overhead. One was a life flight, the other police. Jared was the first to break away from them and race to the melee, Alexander close behind.

When the rest of them reached the area where their sons were, they heard one of the cops say they had two dead, both males, and that no one could enter until the FBI was finished.

"Willow? Willow James, is she in there? Please, you have to tell me," Jared begged the officer. "She's his sister and my fiancée."

"I'm sorry, sir, I can't give you—" he was cut off by another man, this one in a suit.

"I'll talk to him." He waited until the officer walked away. "If you folks will step over here, I can give you what I can."

J.R. held his wife as Edgar did the same to Amanda. They were led past a tarp-covered lump and overheard one of the men standing next to it say "bled to death" before they were escorted to an area just behind the trailer.

"My name is Agent Samuel Gant with the FBI. What I'm going to tell you is strictly off the record and will be my ass if you repeat any of it. The girl is in bad shape. The medics don't know the extent of her injuries because...because one of the bastards nailed her leg to the floor. They are bringing in a crew to cut the flooring away because they don't know for sure if the nails being removed would cause her more damage than just leaving them for the hospital to take care of. The team is about twenty minutes away and—"

"I'll do it," Jared said to him. "I'm a carpenter and I have the knowledge of every piece of equipment used here. Let me do it for her."

Amanda started to say something, but Edgar pulled her back. J.R. wasn't so sure it was a good idea either. Jared loved this woman and if anything happened to her because he'd caused it, J.R. knew he'd never forgive himself.

Gant looked back at the building before he answered Jared. "If she doesn't get help soon, she'll die. You understand that, right? The medics are saying even if they get her to a hospital soon…it just might be for nothing. She's lost a great deal of blood, young man."

"I want to do this. Please, I have to try." J.R. took a deep breath when he heard the pain in his son's voice

After a moment's hesitation, Jared was escorted to the building. After only a few steps Jared returned and pulled Amanda James into his arms and hugged her. "I'll make her live. I'll make sure he knows I won't let her die." Releasing her, he ran to the officer.

J.R. had never been more proud of his son in all his life.

~Chapter 21~

Jared followed the agent toward the building. He tried to think what the fuck had gotten into him when they were suddenly inside. The place was bright with lights from the cruisers and medical teams. Someone had even plugged in the heavy duty construction lights as well. He was led up to the third floor.

There was a tarp covering something near the broken out window at the front of the building. Since it was covered in blood, Jared assumed it was another corpse like the one in the lot. Around the room were several yellow little tent like markers, most of them by the body, a few more near the broken glass. Jared didn't see Willow right away.

The medic team was close to the wall and the police, two of them had their guns out but at their sides. They seemed to be guarding the medics.

With a quiet "wait here," Agent Gant went to the team. Within seconds, two of them stood and he could finally see her.

Someone had removed one leg of her pants and she lay bare from her panties to her foot. Her leg was at an odd angle and from where he stood, all he could see was blood and lots of it.

Her shirt sleeves had been cut open and Jared could make out in IV in her arm. The front of her shirt was pulled up or cut away, he couldn't tell which, but he could see her exposed belly and the bruising there. There were also a few bloodied places there as well. But it was her face that made him need to find the bastard who'd hurt her and beat the ever-loving shit out of him.

Both her eyes were swollen, one completely closed. Her lower lip looked like someone had bitten her. The long cut in her forehead was open and one of the medics was wiping it with a white cloth. Jared wondered if that was how her blood had ended up on the door at the hotel where she'd been staying.

Jared suddenly hoped that one of the two tarps held the dead bastard that had hurt her because if not, then he would wish that he was. Whoever had dared do this to his love wasn't going to be long for this world anyway. Jared looked at Agent Gant when he returned.

"The medic said he'd hold her still while you cut her free. He doesn't think she'll wake, but he said she will still feel the pain and will scream. He wants to make sure that you'll be able to handle that."

Could he? Probably not, but he wasn't going to stop now. Before he could think about it anymore, he nodded to the agent.

"Good. Do you have any questions?" Jared shook his head then nodded.

"Yes. I'd like…can I call my parents? I want to assure them that she's here. That I have her." he wanted to give them comfort, but the agent warned him not to give them any details.

"We don't want them to come up here just yet. We're still processing the scene. It may take us a while to…your girl there? We think she might have stopped the biggest crime lord in the United States. She took him out with a nail gun."

Jared looked back at Willow then at the agent. "Sounds like something she'd do." He stepped closer to her and pulled out his cell phone. His father answered on the first ring. Jared had never been so glad to hear his voice in his life.

"Dad—" Emotion swamped him. Tears fell freely down his cheeks and he choked on a sob. "Tell them…tell them it's her. Tell them that I have her and that…and that I'll try my best for her."

"We know that, son. And Jared…I love you with all my heart. Take care of your girl."

Jared set to work. He took a large circular saw and cut a two foot long seam about three inches on either side of her thigh. The medic with him, Tyler Landis, had covered Willow's wound up with large gauze then wrapped a thermo blanket over her body. When he covered her face, Jared had a moment of panic and asked him to please pull it off her. Tyler started to protest, but in the end decided to simply do as Jared had asked. He was glad; he really would have hated to hurt the guy. The blanket over her face looked too much like the other two tarps for his taste.

He tried not to think about what he was doing or for that matter, who he was doing it for. Instead, he concentrated on the task and not the why. It took him only fifteen minutes to cut the seams.

"We have to set her up to cut in the other direction. The hospital wants as little as possible of the floor brought with her. Once we get everything cut down, then five men plus you and I are going to pry the flooring up and they'll take her away."

Jared nodded. He was missing something here, but he couldn't tell what. Something about the way the guy kept stalling. Then he remembered what the agent had said.

"I know it will hurt her. I'm aware that she'll be screaming."

Tyler nodded. "Yes, you've been told she'll scream, but do you know how much? Mr. Stone, she is going to scream in pain and she is going to do it the entire time it takes us to finish this. Scream for us to stop, scream for her mother and dad. You have no idea what it's like to know that you can't help her and neither can we. I want you to know that it's necessary. I promise you it will only get better once we get her to the hospital."

Jared looked at him then at Willow. "You're afraid I'll hit you, aren't you?"

"Yes, sir, I am. I've been in this situation before. I know you won't mean to, but you're a big man and, well...I don't want to have to have one of those cops shoot you to stop you from hurting me."

Jared looked at the police standing there. Tyler had a point. He didn't know what it was going to be like and all he could do was promise him he'd try not to hit him. Tyler nodded and stuck out his hand.

"Good luck, Mr. Stone. Now let's cut this bastard."

Tyler was right. Jared wasn't prepared. Her screams pounded in his head as he ran the saw. It seemed an eternity before he got the first seam cut and longer for the second, even though it was the same length. When the other men came forward with their pry bars and they stuck them in the cuts, he thought he'd puke when blood began pooling beneath the boards and over her. Still she screamed and sobbed.

She'd begged them to stop, begged him to please make them stop. She called for her dad and her mom. She yelled for Alexander as well. Then she was free.

Jared was drenched in sweat despite the cold air. Even as he followed her gurney down the stairs, he wanted to pull her into his arms and simply comfort her. He was weak and dizzy by the time they got down the stairs.

Willow was loaded into an ambulance that was taking her to an open field where it would take her to the nearest hospital. They told him that she would be at the hospital and in surgery before they got there.

Their families met him right outside the door when they came out. Her parents followed as far as the ambulance then came back to him. His dad was telling him something when he realized he'd missed it.

"...the driver take us straight to the hospital. The police had kindly offered their help as an escort." his dad stressed the word "kindly" and Jared knew that he'd called in a favor. "The helicopter is taking her straight to Ohio State University Medical Center.

We'll more than likely be there after she's in surgery."

Jared got into the car and laid his head back. She would be fine, she would be fine. He had to believe that or he would go insane.

~oOo~

Willow woke again. She remembered the first time and even the second time because of the pain, the incredible pain. She still hurt, but she knew better than to move this time. She figured as long as she was still, she'd not hurt. At least not much.

Sounds. She could hear the squeak of shoes, faint and distant. A bell sounded from far away almost like chimes then an announcement telling people thanks for coming but visiting hours were over. She could smell things too. The harsh odor of disinfectants, food over cooked, and the tinny smell of blood all mingled together into the horrific smells of a hospital.

Her leg hurt, but she couldn't move her toes. She had a moment of panic about that, but didn't want to think about what might be wrong. She knew they were still there; she had rubbed them together the first time she'd awakened. Phantom pain had her taking a deep breath and she discovered pain there as well.

Willow still hadn't opened her eyes, but she could tell that the room was dark. She knew that sooner rather than later she'd have to, but not just yet. She continued her inventory of her body.

Bypassing her toe wiggling for the moment, she moved her fingers one at a time. When she reached the eighth one, she felt something attached to it...something like a clamp. She wasn't overly concerned. She could move her finger, it was just very heavy. The rest of her fingers were fine.

She was exhausted by the time she was finished. Her ribs were sore and hurt like hell when she took a deep breath. Her head hurt too, but nothing she couldn't stand. There was a tightness in her throat, but again, nothing she couldn't manage. Now all she had to do was open her eyes.

The room was large and the dim light behind her illuminated it just enough that she could make out things. She'd knew she'd been at a hotel, that there were some children and then lots of pain. She knew she was in a private room in a hospital. She even remembered why...a little of it anyway.

When she tried to focus too hard on what had happened, she got sharp pains in her head for her trouble. It would come back to her, she was sure. What she wasn't sure of was whether or not she wanted it to.

There was a couch just to her right that was occupied. By whom she couldn't tell. An overstuffed chair, also occupied, was near it. There were other shapes, a table with something on it, another chair, bunches of tall and short bushy things that she surmised were flowers from their smell. Willow looked down at herself.

She wasn't surprised by the sheets, or the smallish hospital bed. But by the head attached to very broad shoulders, she was. It was a startling contrast from his dark hair to the whiteness of the sheets.

Jared. She got a pain in her head when she tried to think about him. Something had happened, something at her house, but she couldn't remember. Closing her eyes to try and calm the pounding, she fell back to sleep when the headache lessened a bit.

The next time she woke, the room was brighter. She still didn't move her body much, but did open her eyes. The bunches were flowers, and lots of them. Some were huge while others were small plants. The couch was empty, but the chair wasn't. Her dad sat there asleep.

She felt tears well in her eyes looking at him. When had he grayed so much? Had he always been that way? Willow didn't think so. She could hear him snore now, and thought what a comfort it was to her. The soft inhales of air and the hard rumbling of him exhaling made her smile. He'd been telling her mom for years that he most certainly didn't snore.

There was a man sitting in the other chair. Willow was sure that she didn't know him. There was no pain associated with trying to remember. He was awake and reading something and only looked up at her when a nurse walked in the room.

Her badge said her name was Debbie, RN. Her crisp uniform, a startling white against her dark skin, was also a giveaway. She didn't look at Willow as she wrapped the cuff of the blood pressure equipment around Willow's arm. It wasn't until she was pumping it up that she looked up and made eye contact.

Willow might have laughed at her expression if she wasn't afraid that it would hurt. She had to lick her lips twice before she could speak to her.

"Where?" It was the best she could manage and even that was exhausting. But it seemed to wake Debbie up.

"OSU Med Center. You...Glad your back." The smile was huge and Debbie, now that she wasn't in shock any longer, became a chatter box as she continued with her task. "You've been here for nine days. Only in this room for three. Intensive care, you know. You have some muscle damage to your thigh, but you do the PT stuff and you'll not have much of a limp. The crease in your head isn't so bad now. You should have seen it when they brought you in. Woo doggie, it was ugly."

Willow looked around the room. The man she didn't recognize was shaking her dad awake. And when he looked where the man had nodded, she burst into tears.

"Daddy." The pain disappeared when he came to her, everything came into focus, and she thought the world was back where it should be.

"Oh my baby girl. My baby girl." He touched her gently, but he didn't hug her. She was glad that he remembered her injuries because she would have leapt out of the bed and into his arms had he not stopped her. As it was, she was already sore.

She wasn't sure how long they sat there, not saying anything aside from her assuring him she was fine now. He didn't mention how she'd managed to get hurt and she didn't ask what had happened.

The door to her room opened again and the stranger and another man came in. She hadn't even realized the man had even left. Neither man said much to her or her dad, but they did seem to have a great deal to say to each other. She and her dad ignored them both.

When the door opened again, J.R. Stone, Mrs. Stone, Willow's mother and brother both came in along with Jared. Her mother took her hand and her brother stood close to her bed. They were all talking all at once, everyone but Jared. He stood close to the two men and stared at her. When yet another man came into the room, everyone suddenly stopped talking as he walked up to the foot of her bed. She knew that whatever he said she was not going to like.

"Hello, Miss James. These men are with the FBI. My name is Agent Gant and this man is Agent Wilson. They want to ask you some questions about the two men that were killed the night you were kidnapped and injured."

And just like that, with amazing clarity and a great many details, it all came rushing back to her.

~Chapter 22~

Jared watched her face while she talked with his family and hers. She was confused, he could see, and she kept looking his way. He wanted to tell everyone to leave them alone, but knew that the family, especially hers, needed this. He was actually waiting until the Feds showed up anyway.

When Agent Gant showed up just before the attorney that his dad had gotten for her, Jared noticed that he looked grim. Jared had spoken to the man several times over the past week and he genuinely liked the guy.

He introduced everyone to Willow and Jared saw the exact moment that she remembered. Her face crumpled and her eyes darted around the room. When she looked at him, he stepped toward her.

Her face was pale, paler than when he'd come in. The light color she'd had in her cheeks while talking had faded when her memories returned. She looked afraid, terror lurked in her eyes. He could see her uncertainty and that shocked him most of all. This was not his Willow.

Taking her hand into his, he looked her in the eyes. "You didn't do anything wrong, Willow."

He wasn't getting through and she was starting to hyperventilate. He squeezed her hand and threw himself on the blade so to speak. "I should have told you who I was." her confusion seemed to fade a bit. "After we made love, I should have told you who I was."

"You mean after you fucked me."

He started to laugh, but was afraid she'd slug him. She certainly recovered fast.

"You were a good lay, what can I say?" He heard her father rumble something. "Willow, you don't believe that any more than I do."

He saw her stiffen then wince, but she didn't back off. "Are you saying I wasn't a good lay, Jared Robert Stone? Because you know damn good and well I was the best you've ever had."

Her eyes sparkled, whether from anger or mischief he didn't know, or care. Jared heard his dad laugh then try to cover it with a cough.

"Maybe. But then we really didn't get to…practice very much, did we?"

Alexander grabbed his shoulder as Jared spoke to Willow. "Maybe you should back the fuck away from my little sister."

Jared didn't take his eyes from Willow's. She looked at him too. When Alexander tried to push him off the bed, Willow finally spoke up. "You're a real bastard, you know that?" He nodded at her and smiled. "Let him go, Alexander. Mr. Stone is just trying to piss me off."

"What the fuck, Wills? This man just insulted you, he lied to you, and now he's telling you…he's saying that… Damn it, Wills, if I had known what kind of man he really was, I wouldn't have helped him find you." Alexander let Jared go. "This is stupid."

"Miss James, while this has been very...educational, there are some—"

"Shut up, Wilson." Jared didn't need to turn to see Gant was pissed. He could hear it in his voice as he spoke to his partner. "Can't you see these two are working things out? Miss James, when you're up to it, I'd like to ask you a few questions."

"It's Willow, and now is fine. Let's get this over with. And Mr. Stone and I"—she jerked her hands from his—"are finished."

Jared stood up and leaned down to her, face bracing his hands on either side of her. He brought his mouth to just brushing hers before he spoke. He watched, mesmerized, as her tongue flicked out and ran quickly over her lush lips. Hunger for a taste nearly made him whimper.

"Oh we're far from finished, Willow. Very far." He gave in then and brushed his mouth over hers. Once, twice, then again before he kissed her.

Her mouth opened under his, her tongue slid along his, and that did make him moan. When her fingers curled around his arm, he deepened the kiss more, eating at her soft lips and dueling with her tongue. Need coiled around him and centered in his groin. Reluctantly, he pulled back, remembering her injuries and the people in the room before he did something really stupid and begged her to take him.

Standing again, he nearly did beg, nearly snarled at them all to get out and to leave them alone for a few minutes, no, a few hours...days...weeks...years. Even then he wasn't sure that would be enough time. She looked...beautiful came to mind, but it seemed so unimaginative. Delicious and soft, sexy and erotic all came to mind when he looked down at her.

With a quick kiss to her nose and a "mine," he walked to the couch and sat down. It was either that or fall on his face. Every drop of his blood had pooled in his cock.

~oOo~

Everyone cleared out of the room except for the two agents and the man Mr. Stone Sr. had introduced as her attorney, Andrew Gibson, and of course Jared. He said he wasn't leaving and no one argued with him overly much. Not even her glaring at him did anything other than make him laugh at her. She decided to make him pay later.

The questions were hard to answer for the most part. Why did Talbor target her? Did she know the other man there? Did she know if he was alone? But the hardest ones to answer, the last ones, made her uncomfortable.

"Did you see Smith kill Talbor?" Gant asked her twice when she didn't answer right away.

She looked into Jared's eyes as she spoke. "Yes. It was…I hurt so badly by then, but I could see them both. He had…Smith had already shot him, Talbor I mean. He shot him in the belly. I didn't hear it, but I saw Talbor drop and clutch…his belly was covered in blood."

"Did he say anything?" Gant asked her softly. "Either man, did they say anything to each other?"

"Mr. Smith was pissed. He wanted to know where his merchandise was. I think he was mad mostly because Talbor kept calling it drugs. He told him, Mr. Smith told him that he'd…" She looked up at Gant. "Mr. Smith told Talbor that if he hadn't already killed his predecessor that he'd find him again and kill him all over for hiring Talbor in the first place."

Gant stopped writing in his notebook. "Did he mention his name? Did Talbor say his name?"

Willow looked back at Jared fleetingly then at the floral arrangement on the table. Jared looked upset and she wondered what he would think of her when he found out she had murdered someone.

"He had already put the gun in his mouth and killed him by then. He was sorta talking to himself, I think. No, He didn't...Smith didn't say his name."

Gant shifted. "Willow, this is a question I don't want you to answer without conferring with your attorney first." She knew what the agent was going to ask her and she was going to answer. She'd answer as soon as she could get her heart to stop pounding.

"Willow, did you kill Daniel Smith?"

Willow lay back on the pillows while Mr. Gibson argued with the two agents. She felt the bed shift and knew without opening her eyes that it was Jared. When he laced his fingers with hers, she relaxed. She had no idea why she found that comforting, but it was. When he ran his fingers up and down her arm, Willow felt her body begin to settle, become soft, and before she knew it, she was asleep.

It was dark in the room when she woke the next time. She moved her uninjured leg before she thought and was surprised at how little it hurt. She lifted her arm that wasn't attached to the IV and it felt better too.

"You've healed quite a bit in the last several days. I'm glad. I hated seeing you in pain."

Willow looked over at Mrs. Stone. Then around the room. They were alone. And not only alone, but the door was shut too. Willow turned the light over her head on and looked at her, wondering what she could possibly want.

"I've asked them to go and get some dinner. I told them I'd be happy to sit with you." She smiled at Willow. "I'd hope you'd wake so we could talk."

"Mrs. Stone, I'm very sorry about all this. I never meant for this—"

"Sorry for what, dear? Having a madman hurt you? Having been kidnapped? I hardly think any of that was any fault of yours." She pinned Willow with a look. "Unless of course you're sorry for the affair you're having with my son."

Willow flushed. "I'm not having an affair with Jared. And whatever we had...did is over. It was just sex. Nothing more. He's...he doesn't mean...I don't mean anything to him."

"Hummm, I would say that's not true and that you know it. Jared is in love with you. And if the way you look at him is any indication, I'd say you love him too. Do you?"

Willow looked away. Mrs. Stone was seeing entirely too much. And she didn't... no, she couldn't love him. He'd lied to her.

"I've fallen in love with your house." Willow looked at her again. "Your parents insisted that we stay there with them. Jared has been making use of that beautiful kitchen or yours. Marta said you've never used it."

"I don't cook. She does it when it suits her. She tends to be more bossy than—" Willow stopped. "Thank you."

Mrs. Stone nodded as if she knew what Marta was like. "Jared has always wanted a house with a huge kitchen. He'd like to raise lots of children in his kitchen. Do you want children? Marta was telling us what else you're planning for it. I can't wait to see it when it's complete."

Willow nodded then shook her head. She wasn't sure what she was saying yes or no to, but her head was beginning to spin. "I only work on it when I have some spare time. The bedrooms on the second floor are taking—he doesn't love me. You're mistaken about that."

"Marta is a dream. I've been trying to steal her away, but she won't budge. And those sticky buns she makes are to die for. Yes, he does. Do you think I could get a copy of the recipe when you marry Jared?"

Willow stared at her for several seconds. The changes in subjects were making her crazy. She was having trouble keeping up.

"It's a family recipe. Her mom works for my parents. What do you mean marry—I'm not marrying anyone. Especially not...he hasn't asked me ye—" Willow took a deep breath. "You know what? This conversation is over, Mrs. Stone."

She just laughed. "Perhaps you should call me by my first name, dear. 'Mrs. Stone' could get rather confusing at the family get-togethers. My first name is Slade."

Willow stared at her, waiting for her to say she was kidding. When she didn't, Willow started to giggle. "Your name is Slade Stone."

"Yes. My father wanted a son. I was his last chance at naming a child after him. I have six sisters all with very girly girl names." Slade was laughing now too.

Willow knew it was going to hurt, knew as sure as she laid there she was going to regret it, but could no more stop the laughter that burst out than she could breath.

And that was how Jared found them when he walked in later. Both of them with tears on their cheeks while someone from the nursing staff was trying to get her to eat some lime Jell-o and tepid tea.

~Chapter 23~

His mother left an hour later. Willow and she seemed to be getting along, but he knew his mother was a great person and could charm anyone into anything. Jared watched as Willow tried to struggle with the sheets before he finally got up and began straightening them for her.

"I can do it. Just go home. To your home, why don't you? I have nurses here if I need something."

Prickly. He could handle that. It was the indifference that he hated. He smiled at her as he sat down on the sheets and trapped her hands beneath them. She looked up at him with a huff.

"I want to talk to you about something. You and I are long overdue for a—stop fighting me and sit still." She was trying to get out from under the sheet. "Willow, look at me."

"I want you to go. I don't want you here. And I've got that thingy with the Feds in the morning and I need my rest. Your mom said that you are in charge of the site now and they start to work—"

He kissed her quiet. It had the desired effect, but some of it back fired too. He loved this woman and he wanted her to know it. When the kissed ended, much too soon for his thinking, she lay back against the bed again.

"Why do you keep doing that? You and I are not going to be seeing one another after this thing tomorrow so I'd like for you to stop doing that." She wouldn't look at him.

He laughed and she snorted at him. He'd heard her dad do the same and wondered who had taught who that. There were a lot of things he wanted to know about her. But he had to get over this lie he'd told her.

"Willow, Talbor got to Conley and his family." her eyes jerked up to his. "Thomas and his wife are in the hospital. His children are being cared for by his mom. But everyone is going to be okay. One of his kids, the oldest I think, got up to go to the bathroom and saw the light on in the living room. He called nine-one-one when he…Talbor had beaten his dad up pretty good, and his mom…Mrs. Conley had been beaten too, but not as badly."

"And the other kids? Molly and Blake, are they all right too?" Jared nodded. "Thank goodness. Why? Why did he hurt her and him?"

Jared stood up and toed off his shoes. "I don't know. She said that he kept asking her for keys. Said you'd hidden them from him and he needed them."

"He asked me about keys too. He kept telling me he only had so much time and that he needed the keys." he watched as she licked her lips. "What are you doing?"

The chimes sounded then a soft bell through the quiet of the room. Jared looked at his watch as the announcement was made that visiting hours were over and thanked people for coming in. Jared started on the buttons of his shirt.

"I'm tired. I thought we'd make an early night of it before you have the rest of your interview in the morning." He laid his shirt over the back of the chair. "Agent Gant said he'd be here by nine." He walked over to the little nightstand and began empting his pockets. He hesitated about taking out the jewelers box and decided now was not the time to propose. She was still a little mad at him.

"You can't...what do you think you're doing? You have to leave. I want you to leave. Now. I have nothing more to say to you." her grip on the sheet had her knuckles white and her voice cracked a bit. "I thank you for the information about Conley, but you need to leave."

Jared handed her the slip of paper he'd asked his mom to get for him. It stated that he could stay after visiting hours and that the staff was to accommodate him and Willow in whatever they needed.

"This doesn't say you can sleep in here. Nor does it mention you needing to be naked either. Dress and get the hell out of here." She was panicky again. He refrained from pointing that out to her.

He simply looked at her as he pulled off his belt. There was no way he was leaving here before morning. And especially not until he could convince her to marry him and soon. He grinned when he thought about what his mother had told him when she handed him the permission.

"You make this work with her or so help me Jared, I will disown you and adopt her. Right now I like her a damn sight better than I do you. I will be extremely disappointed in you if you can't convince her that you love her."

He laid the belt on the chair. "I'm not going anywhere. Scoot over some. These beds are much too small for two people." He unbuttoned his pants and lowered the zipper as he sat on the edge of the bed. "Here and It are with Alexander by the way. And I took them to their vet appointment. I didn't know they were purebloods and not related. That's awesome."

"The idiot who named them bought them to breed. And—why did you take them? They don't like to ride in strangers' cars. Marta has to fight to get them in her car." She looked ready to cry. "They don't like strangers' cars."

"Honey, I bribed them. I gave them a slice of bacon when they got in and then when we got finished with the vet. Now every time I open the door, I have to drag them out again. It was a mistake with the bacon, I'll admit that now." She smiled a watery smile at him and he felt like such a heel. "Are you going to move over or do you plan to take up all the bed?"

"Jared, please? I don't want…You have to go before you break my heart. I know you don't…I know you won't ever love again and I can be okay with that as long as you leave now." He didn't know what she was talking about. "Your leg."

Love his leg again? Then she pointed to his calf. He looked down at the long forgotten tattoo. He took the sheet from her hand and climbed into the bed with her. After getting her comfortable, he wrapped his arms around her gently and pulled her into his arms.

"I was seventeen and she was…she was considerably older so she broke my heart—or as broken as a horny teenager can have their heart broken. She'd seduced me, easily, I suppose. Anyway, I was having the affair of a lifetime and thought I'd found my true love. Turned out she was married." He felt her stiffen beside him and nearly laughed. "She had kids my age."

She turned to look at him. He could see the anger there in her eyes and was pleased by it. That was until he realized that the anger was directed at him.

"You should be horsewhipped. That poor woman—"

"Poor woman?" He sat up. "She seduced me. I'm the one who got his heart broken. I'm the—"

"Oh poo. You could charm the panties off a nun and you know it. Of all the...did you expect me to be sorry about it for you?"

Jared wasn't sure whether he should be happy or insulted by her assessment of him. Before he could say anything else, she continued.

"I suppose you were drunk when you got that sappy tat, too." He didn't answer because she was right. "If you think that every time we fight you're going to get yourself inked, well, you can just forget about using my kitchen. Do you hear me?"

It took him several seconds for his head to catch up with what she was saying. Then when he did, he couldn't hide the hope in his voice. "Willow? Are you asking me to move in with you?" His heart hammered in his chest waiting for her answer.

She took her time. She settled into the bed and pulled the sheet up and over them both. Then she fussed with the blanket before she reached over and turned off the light. The room was plunged in darkness.

"If you want. Your mom said...she said that you'd been using the kitchen anyway. Marta claims you're a good cook." Her voice was low and soft. "And the dogs seem to like you."

He waited for what seemed an eternity. What for, he wasn't sure, but he knew that there was more. She had more to tell him.

"And you, Willow? Do you like me too?" He took her hand in his as he waited for an answer.

"Sometimes. Mostly I...mostly, I love you. I know we've not really known each other all that long and I know I'm really inexperienced wh—where are you going now?"

He went to his pants and got out the little box. Then he stood next to the bed "Turn on the light please." She turned on the light to dim. "More." The room brightened and she had tears in her eyes.

Going down on one knee near the bed, he took her hand in his again. Ignoring her protests, he opened the box and showed her what was nested inside. Her "oh my" gave him courage.

"Willow James, will you please marry me? Marry me so I can make love with you every night and every morning? Will you marry me so that I can cook you wonderful meals in your kitchen? I want you to marry me so that I can stand on our deck and shout 'Come Here, Damn It' to our dogs. But mostly, will you marry me because I love you with every part of my body, my heart, and my soul?" He stood when she didn't answer right away.

"You're insane. Do you know that? You make me nuts too. Marry you? Do you know that any children we have are going to need to be watched so that they don't pick up any of your—"

He kissed her. She'd said yes. Even if she didn't say the actual word, he was taking her comment about children as a yes. Pulling back just enough to look at her, he grinned at her dazed expression.

"I love you, Willow." He took the ring out of the box and put it on the tip of her ring finger. "Will you let me dress your finger?"

"Will you have that ridiculous tattoo removed?" Jared nodded. "Then yes, you can dress my finger."

After slipping the ring onto her left hand, he kissed her again. He was hers. Smiling, he climbed back into her bed and held her. It wasn't long before they were both asleep.

~*Chapter 24*~

Samuel looked down at the couple in the bed. They were so wrapped up around each other it was difficult to tell which limb beneath the covers belonged to which one of them. He was loath to wake them, but needed to get this finished once and for all. He wanted to get back to his own office.

"Mr. Stone, Jared? Willow?" Neither of them woke, but they did stir. It wasn't until he said their names twice more that Jared opened his eyes.

"Hello, Samuel. How's it going? Is it that late already?" Jared stretched and looked at his watch. Then he woke Willow. "I suppose you're here to take her statement early, huh?"

"Yes. Something like that." Samuel pulled one of the chairs over and sat down. "I was really worried Danny told you who his contact was, his boss I mean. But I guess he didn't, did he?"

"Danny? Oh, you mean Daniel Smith. No, he didn't. I thought you'd already been told I didn't know." Willow sat up in bed more.

A little nurse walked in just as he was getting ready to ask them questions. She smiled at him. Samuel loved pretty women and this little nurse was beautiful. She seemed a little startled, but he told her that he wanted to get this over with so that he could get back to work.

"And if you don't mind, do you think we could have a couple of hours without any interruptions? I have some questions to ask them and it's easier if there aren't people coming in and out disturbing us."

Nurse Peggy, her tag said. "Sure. Just let us know when you're all finished in here and we'll know when to take Miss James to x-ray."

"And Talbor didn't mention anyone's name," Willow continued when Peggy was gone. "He didn't even say Mr. Smith's name. Did you want to ask me those questions now?"

Samuel grinned. They still didn't have a clue. Oh well, it was quieter this way, he supposed. He decided to play for a bit longer.

"No need. I've got all the answers already. Danny was a good drug lord, if a bit on the naive side. He should have gotten rid of you when he first found you there. He'd still be alive if he had." Jared moved to get up. "No, you don't want to do that. Just wait right there. I've got your demises all planned out."

"Demises? I don't under...Jared?" Willow sounded scared. Good, he thought. He liked a little terror with his murder. Otherwise, what was the point?

"He's the boss. Samuel Gant is...was Daniel's boss, and he's here to kill us. Aren't you?" Jared was a bright boy.

"Why? What possible reason could you have to kill us now?" Willow sat up in bed. "You know, this is really shitty. I could have gone my whole entire life without ever knowing who you were and now you decide to kill us."

Samuel laughed. "And what would be the fun in that, my dear? There—" Willow cut him off.

"I'm not your 'dear,' you fucking prick." Fire burned from her eyes. Samuel could feel a hard-on coming on. He loved beggars when he murdered, but this woman was proving that he liked them spicy too.

"Willow, perhaps you shouldn't piss off the man with the gun. He may shoot us," Jared warned her.

"That's a good boy, calm the girl down. But just so we're clear, I'm killing you anyway. It's only fair. She killed my son, and now I get to kill you." He had their attention now. "Yes, you see Danny Prescott was my son and I had worked very hard to groom him into position. Then you had to come along and murder him. He—"

"Murder him? In case you missed something, he was planning to kill me after he'd killed Talbor." Samuel was beginning to hate this woman.

"Shut up, bitch. Son, you'd better curb your girl there or you won't know why I have to kill you both." Samuel sat on the edge of his chair. "Where was I? Oh yeah, grooming. Danny was a good boy, but he lacked discipline. He finally came into his own right after he killed his brother. Nasty business that. Anyway, you killed him."

He waited for her to say she was sorry. She should, he figured. But when she only glared at him, he decided that he was killing her last. And he was going to make it painful.

"I went up there to see what was taking him so long. Danny should have been finished with Talbor. When I was about halfway up the stairs, I heard a crash. I couldn't believe he'd fallen like that. By the time I got to his body, he'd already bled out. I didn't know you were up there until that fucking bastard Agent Gant showed up. Then by the time I'd gotten rid of his body, the fucking stupid police showed up too. I'm just one lucky bastard that none of the other men had ever seen Gant, only spoken to him on the phone. He told me that before I killed him. One of them cocksuckers that were supposed to be guarding Danny called them."

"Your name isn't Gant. You're Donald Prescott." Jared only looked at him. "All this time you've been…Christ, you meant to let her die. Before you took me up there, you meant for Willow to die."

"You're a smart boy. Yeah. I told that team of workers not to hurry, that we needed to clear the scene anyway. But you had to volunteer. Nearly had your idea vetoed, but one of the local yokels recognized you and before I knew it, you were cutting her loose."

Willow started crying. Tears from a woman didn't faze him at all. All it did was piss him off. Donald pointed the gun at her, but Jared's next statement made him smile. Donald loved a good adversary.

"You were going to kill her the other night when my mom was here. She said you were somewhat short with her." Jared laughed, but there was little humor in it. "My mother said she didn't trust you at all."

Donald bristled at that. There was no way she'd known. He was a charmer and he liked women to fawn over him. If he remembered correctly, she had been short with him.

"Yeah, I was just gonna finish them both off, but that nurse came in too. It's like fucking Grand Central around here." Donald stood. "It is time to go now. I only told the nurses I needed a couple of hours. Gotta make my escape."

He walked to the bed and put his gun toward Jared's head. He winked at him.

The noise behind him was unexpected. He turned and dropped his gun to his side. Fucking people, didn't they know—

"Police. Hands up."

The first bullet hit him in the chest and knocked him into the little night stand. When the second one hit his shoulder, he dropped the gun. He looked to the doorway and saw that pretty little nurse from earlier. And she had her gun pointed at him.

Donald reached for his fake ID. Pain exploded in his face. Now he couldn't see anything as he dropped to the floor and onto his knees. He heard screaming and would have told them to shut the fuck up, but couldn't make his mouth work. Pain seemed to hit him in waves. Before he hit the floor completely, he realized he was dead, as dead as dead could be.

~Chapter 25~

The police were everywhere. Willow just watched them process everything and didn't say much unless they specifically asked her something.

She'd already figured out a lot. The police had suspected Samuel...Donald would come in and kill her. So they had bugged her room. She looked up to where they had told her the camera had been. Her mind kept going around and around on the fact that she could have gotten someone...namely Jared, killed.

The police officer that had shot Donald Prescott had told her that they'd put it in there when she'd gone down for an x-ray the other morning. Willow hadn't had any, of course. They'd shuffled her around until she was in so much pain all she wanted them to do was shoot her. She stopped that thought immediately.

Jared had had to put on a gown when they'd let him and her move around. Well, he moved, she was just put into another bed and pushed against the far wall out of the way of the forensic personnel. Now he was in a pair of scrubs. She'd almost gotten him killed. She glanced at the wall that had been splattered with blood, but someone had closed the curtain. It had sprayed the white wall like an abstract painting. She looked up as the doctor came toward her.

"Miss James, we're going to move you now. Your parents are there waiting for you." he was checking her pulse while he talked to her. She could feel his fingers resting there. "I've arranged for you to have a sedative when you want it. You've had an ordeal today."

She could only smile at his description. Yeah, it had been an ordeal. This whole month had been an ordeal.

Willow only nodded. She had made her own arrangements. She was moving down the hall toward the other room when two men, Sherman and Thomason, walked up beside her and took the bed she was in from the orderly who was pushing it.

"You know, Will, I don't think this is such a good idea. You know that…well, things are gonna hit the fan when someone finds out you has gone missing." Thomason nodded at Sherman's statement. "And I'd just as soon not be on the receiving end of that man."

"I don't want you to get into trouble over me, Sherman. You can just take me to the ambulance then I can take it from there. I almost got him killed today and I…I can't do that to him again." She had to fight the tears. "This will be better for everyone."

"I know you wouldn't. But you see…well, when you texted me…well, there was…we wasn't—fuck, Will."

She closed her eyes, knowing she wasn't going to like where this was going. "Was Alexander with you?" Sherman nodded and so did Thomason. "And he knows?" Again, they nodded.

She was nearly to the elevator when she saw Sherman stiffen and Thomason step away. With a quick "sorry Will," both men stepped into the elevator and left her there. She turned to see the man standing next to her and he didn't look all that happy with her.

"I can explain. I was just—"

"Oh I heard what you were just thinking you were going to do. You were going to leave me. Not happening. I've fallen in love with you and that is all there is to it." Jared moved the bed away from the elevator. "And just so there is no confusion later on, I've taken steps to make things a bit more interesting for us. Well, permanent anyway. And before you get pissed...see that man there? He's clergy. So watch your tongue."

Willow looked to where he had pointed. There was a well-dressed man standing next to her dad and mom. Her mom turned to look when Jared called her name. There were tears in her eyes. As her mom was by the now stopped bed, Jared walked away, but not before kissing her mom on the cheek.

"You should have told me," her mom said as she pulled out her makeup case. "I think it's just wonderful."

Willow was confused until she remembered the ring Jared had given her. She lifted her hand to show her mom and froze at her next statement.

"A baby. That's so wonderful and you dad is over the moon about it. I can't wait. This is a little rushed but—"

Willow put her hand on her mom's to stop her. Willow didn't wear makeup and her mom was an expert. The tiny little brush in her hand was making another pass over her cheeks when she looked at her.

"Baby? I'm not pregnant. Where would you get...I'm going to kill him." She found him looking at her and the arrogant ass winked. "I'm not pregnant, Mom. He lied...Christ, the clergy. You think I'm going to marry him."

"Well of course you are, dear. You are wearing his ring and nowadays no one cares if there are less months between marriage and baby. Hold still." The brush was dipping in for more goop and slathered over her face. Willow was too distracted to stop her.

Her dad thought she was pregnant too. She found him talking to Mr. Stone. Damn it all to hell and back. Jared was going to make her a widow before there really was a kid.

A baby. Jared's and her baby. Willow looked over at him again and wondered what a child of theirs would look like, be like. Beautiful, especially if he looked like his father. She laid her hand over her belly before she could think and heard her mom sniffle. Jerking her hand away, she looked up at her.

"I'm not...Do you think you could get the daddy for me? I'd like to have a few words with him before this fantasy...wedding occurs." She smiled, but didn't fool her mom, apparently.

"Willow, don't hurt him. He means well and it is his child too." She walked away with a huff. Willow thought she heard her say something like she "hoped the baby had his father's temperament," but couldn't be sure.

Jared came toward her after shaking the clergy's hand. She was going to have to go to prison, she just knew it. The man was nuts if he thought he could tell her family...and his apparently, that she was knocked up.

He kissed her quickly on the mouth. "Before you start, let me wheel you in your new room where we'll have some privacy. I'm sure you think you have something to say to me."

She did, but waited. The clergy patted her hand as she went by him and he winked. Was everyone afflicted with something today that made them wink at her? As soon as the door to her room closed, Jared kissed her. And it wasn't like the one in the hall.

His mouth was hot, hard, and wet. His tongue slid along her lips and she opened for him before she could think not to. His body barely touched hers and she could feel the heat from his chest as it brushed over her bare breasts. Need coiled in her and she knew that if she were to let it out, it would pounce on the man before her like a sensual snake. When he pulled back slightly, she was too dazed to think.

"Do you hurt? Your leg, does it hurt right now?" She shook her head. Nothing hurt, but she did ache. "Good. Open your legs for me, I want to touch you."

His voice was low, low and hard. She couldn't have denied him if she tried. Moving her right leg closer to the edge of the bed, he pulled the sheet off her and lifted her gown.

They had removed her catheter that morning and had let her take a shower by setting a chair in the stall and handing her a nozzle. The blood splattered on her was minimal, but she had been able to get cleaned up. It had felt like heaven and she'd stayed a little longer just to wash her entire body twice. The nurse had even helped her wash her hair.

His fingers were gentle as they brushed up and down her thigh. Her pussy tightened in anticipation every time to move closer to it. She canted her hips once and stopped when a small bit of pain lanced across her wound.

"Don't move. Let me do all the work. Christ, I've missed you." his mouth covered hers as he cupped her soft folds.

When his fingers moved under her panties and slid into her, she nearly screamed out from the sensation. In and out he moved inside of her. He pulled his mouth from hers and looked down at what he was doing to her. She looked down too and watched him fuck her like this.

"You've soaked my fingers. And I can feel you tightening around them, pulling them deeper into you. You're so wet, Willow. Wet enough that if I wanted to, I could slide inside of you right now."

She nodded for him to do it. His low chuckle had her look up to his face. He looked in pain, his lips hard, and sweat beaded on his forehead.

"I want you, Jared. Please, I need...I want you." She canted again and if there was pain, she didn't feel it. All she could feel was him and what he was doing to her.

"I can't, baby, not like this. There isn't enough room in this bed and I'd have to be under you so that you don't hurt your leg."

His fingers continued their dance and he leaned over her breast and suckled her through the gown. Reaching up, she unsnapped the arm hole and he groaned as he took her nipple deep into his mouth. When he pulled back, she whimpered.

"Come for me, Willow. Come now." Her body reacted to his command and she bowed her back as his mouth once again covered hers. Even as she screamed out her release, he rode her. When she came again, she thought she had blacked out for a second and opened her eyes and stared up at him.

"What..." She had to clear her throat twice before she could speak. "What about you?"

His head was lying on her shoulder and his fingers were once again stroking her thigh. His hot breath on her bare shoulder was making her needy again and she reached up to curl her hand around his bicep. He looked at her then with a slight moving of his head.

"I ache to be inside of you, love. I want to fuck you so hard that neither of us will walk for a week. But we can't. Not now at any rate." He stood up and she could see the hard outline of his cock at his zipper. "Marry me, Willow. Right now, today. Marry me so that I can keep you with me."

She'd forgotten about that. "Why did you tell them I was pregnant? We both know…my parents, your parents, think that I'm going to have a baby, Jared. What do we say to them when they figure out that it's not going to happen?"

He took her hand in his and kissed it. Then he cupped it over his cock and rocked into it. His moan had her gripping him hard through the soft cotton and he rocked again

"Christ, you're killing me." He pulled her hand away and put it on her lap with exaggerated movements that had her giggle. "This isn't funny. I hurt in any number of places because my balls are blue."

She giggled again and started to reach for him again. He stopped her with a look and a step back. She pouted at him.

"Stop it. About the baby, we won't have to lie to them if you don't want to. It may not come as soon as they think it will, but I'm sure with practice,"—he wiggled his brows at her—"we could produce one soon. I want children with you, Willow. Enough to fill that house of yours, enough that we can fill that kitchen with their friends and our families. Please, say 'I do' to me."

She nodded to him. "Okay, but you're going to have to wait on the actual making part. I can't…I don't think I can have sex just yet."

His smile was pure sin. "Oh, don't worry about that. I've been thinking about how we can have all kinds of kinky sex while you're healing."

Willow was suddenly very nervous as he straightened her gown and the sheets. Then with a quick kiss, he opened the door to their families.

Now Available
Book 2 of The James Children Series

Alexander

About the Author

I woke up one morning and decided to give play time to the people in my head who were keeping me awake. Little did I know that they would be so relentless and want their time right now! I wrote for the pure joy of it and to entertain my family and friends. But mostly it was to get more than an hour of sleep without a story playing out. Of course, the more I write, the more they want. So…well, as a result of sleepless days (I work through the night as a gun toting grandma – nope not a vigilantly but an armed security guard) I have lots of stories written.

Hello! My name is Kathi Barton and I'm an author. I have been married to my very best friend Sonny for at times seems several lifetimes – in a good way, honey. And together we have three wonderful children and then the ones we brought into the world - Paul and Dale Barton, Jason and Wendy Barton and Danielle and Ben Conklin. They have given us seven of the greatest treasures on Earth. They don't live at home seven days a week! No, seriously, seven grandchildren – Gavin, Spring, Ben, Trinity, Sarah, Kelly and Kian.